'Relax.' Griff's deep, velvet voice held a seductive quality that was very hard to resist. 'You're a very attractive woman.'

'Don't!' Ros almost flinched away from him. 'I hate that sort of stupid attempt at flattery.'

A dark flash of annoyance lit his eyes. 'I'm not flattering you,' he retorted bluntly. 'Of course you're not beautiful—I didn't say you were. You don't need to be— the effect you have on men has got nothing at all to do with having a pretty face.'

She felt her cheeks tinge with pink, and looked away from him quickly. 'I...I don't know what you mean,' she protested thickly.

'No?' he laughed softly. 'I don't believe that. I don't think I can be the only one to sense it—it's like a fire inside you.' His hand slid slowly down her back to mould intimately over the base of her spine, holding her far too close for modesty.

LOVE IS FOR THE LUCKY

BY

SUSANNE McCARTHY

MILLS & BOON LIMITED
ETON HOUSE   18-24 PARADISE ROAD
RICHMOND   SURREY   TW9 1SR

First published in Great Britain 1989
by Mills & Boon Limited

© Susanne McCarthy 1989

Australian copyright 1989
Philippine copyright 1989
This edition 1989

ISBN 0 263 76411 7

Set in Times Roman 10½ on 12¼ pt.
01-8909-48800 C

Made and printed in Great Britain

CHAPTER ONE

'In the North there will be more snow over high ground. Many roads over the Pennines are blocked. Police and motoring organisations advise drivers to stay at home unless their journey is absolutely necessary.'

'Thank you', muttered Ros, turning off the car radio. Conditions hadn't been too bad on the motorway—a snow-plough and the weight of traffic had cleared two lanes all the way from Derbyshire, where the snowfall had started. But from the time she had turned off the main road the going had been getting increasingly difficult. And now it was getting dark.

She should be home soon—so long as the car didn't break down. When had she last had it serviced? Not recently, she admitted wryly to herself. It was time she thought about trading it in, really—for one with a decent heater!

She was warm enough, though, huddled up in her serviceable old duffel coat, with a woolly hat pulled down hard over her wild ginger curls. The hands that gripped the steering-wheel were snug in a pair of ancient knitted gloves that she had found—they must have gone through a hole in the pocket of the duffel coat, and been nestling in the lining for years.

She should have stayed in London—one of her old schoolfriends lived there now, and would have gladly put her up. But she had been anxious to get home. She didn't like London at the best of times; she had only gone down to have lunch with her publisher, to celebrate the acceptance of her fourth novel, another political thriller set amid the glitter and intrigue of the court of the first Elizabeth. But something she had read in the paper that morning had given her the germ of an idea for her next plot, and already some complex twists were forming themselves in her mind.

Suddenly a dark figure loomed up in the head-lights. She braked sharply, and the tyres slithered on the ice. It was clear that there had been an accident— she could see the offside rear of a light-coloured car that had run off the road at the bend, and buried itself in a snowdrift. Already the fluttering white flakes were beginning to cover it. Suppressing her natural dislike of strangers, she leaned over and opened the passenger door.

He climbed in stiffly, muttering a thank you in a voice that was thick with cold. He had a black leather travelling-bag that he put on the back seat. Before he closed the door she had a fleeting impression of a tall frame, a dark coat—sheepskin?—with the collar turned up, and damp black hair receding slightly from a high intelligent forehead.

She slid the car into gear, and drove on carefully. Her passenger had stripped off his gloves, and was trying to warm his hands over the inefficient heater-vent. Ros flickered a swift glance at them. They were well-made hands with long, slender fingers, and his wrists were strong with a smattering of dark hair across the backs. But it was his watch that made her look twice—it was either a very expensive Cartier tank-watch or a good fake.

After a while she came to the conclusion that, if she waited for him to start the conversation, she would wait all night, so she asked in a pleasant tone, 'How long have you been there?'

'It seems like hours, but it's probably no more than ten or fifteen minutes.'

The accent was American. What on earth was a rich American doing driving around the wilds of Yorkshire in this weather? It wasn't exactly the tourist season. 'What happened to your car?' she enquired. 'Are you hurt?'

'No, I'm OK. Didn't see the bend,' he answered succinctly.

'It's a bad night to be driving if you don't know the road,' she said. 'It can get nasty up here very suddenly. One minute it's nice and sunny, the next fog or snow comes down and everything grinds to a halt.'

'You'd think the Brits would be ready for it—they do nothing but talk about the weather,' he drawled.

Her eyes flashed indignantly. Damn tourist! She abandoned her attempt to be pleasant, and fixed all her attention on her driving. It was still snowing lightly, and the wind was drifting the snow against the dry-stone walls that lined the road. But she had lived up here in the Yorkshire Dales all her life, and she knew every inch of the way, so she could still make good time.

The man beside her began to seem a little restless. 'Listen, lady, if you don't mind me saying so, do you really have to drive quite so fast?' he enquired.

'It's OK,' she reassured him. 'I know these roads like the back of my hand. And I'd like to get home before the weather gets any worse.'

'Oh-h. Still, if it's all the same to you, I'd kind of like to get home in one piece.'

'What's the matter?' she demanded, needled. 'Don't you trust my driving?'

He shrugged his shoulders. 'I just ain't too keen on women drivers,' he told her bluntly.

Of all the cheek! 'I can assure you, you're perfectly safe with me,' she retorted, an acid edge to her voice. 'I've been driving for years, and I've never had an accident.'

'Well, I guess that might be reassuring,' he drawled lazily. 'But it surely can't have been too many years? What are you—twenty two? Twenty-three?'

'I'm twenty-seven,' she told him coldly, 'and I passed my test when I was seventeen—first time! And if you don't like my driving, you can always get out and walk!' Her anger lent a sharp edge to her voice. If there was one thing she couldn't stand, it was that patronising, 'helpless little woman' attitude. She had to put up with enough of that, living in a small Yorkshire village, where the men still thought they were living in the nineteenth century.

Her passenger seemed to find her annoyance a source of amusement. 'Oh, I don't think I'd care to do that,' he drawled. 'Anyway, you seem to be doing OK so far.'

'Besides, who was the one who drove his car into a snowdrift?' she couldn't resist pointing out.

He chuckled with laughter. *'Touché!'* he acknowledged. 'OK, lady—you drive and I'll shut up.'

Actually, he had quite a nice voice—deep and sort of velvety. She allowed herself to relax a little. 'Where are you going, anyway?' she asked him.

'I'm heading for a place called Arnby Bridge.'

'Arnby Bridge?' She risked taking her eyes off the road for a fraction of a second to try to get a look at his face. 'Why on earth are you going there?'

He smiled at her astonishment. 'I've just bought a house there.'

'So it's you!' There was a note of accusation in her voice that he picked up at once.

'If you're talking about the Priory, then yes, it's me,' he admitted, one eyebrow raised in quizzical enquiry. 'Do you have some objection?'

'What are you going to do with it?' she demanded, her manners forgotten along with her customary shyness.

'Live in it, of course.'

Obviously he hadn't seen it yet! 'It's not been lived in for years,' she warned him.

'Is it haunted?'

'Haunted? Of course not,' she responded, puzzled.

'What a pity.'

She gurgled with laughter. 'What on earth do you want a ghost for?' she enquired cautiously.

'To scare off unwelcome guests.'

'Why don't you just tell them to go away?'

He laughed cynically. 'Oh, if only it were that easy!'

Ros was intrigued. The identity of the Mystery Buyer had been the talk of the whole village for weeks. 'Whatever made you pick Arnby Bridge?' she asked curiously. 'I'm surprised anyone in America has even heard of it.'

'My grandfather was born around here,' he explained. 'His folks took him to America when he was just a kid, but he was always a Yorkshireman at heart—never stopped talking about the place. So when I decided to shift my base of operations to England, it was a natural choice.'

'I don't know if you'll be so keen once you've seen it,' she mused. 'It's a bit off the beaten track.'

'No problem—when the weather's OK I'll be using the chopper to commute.'

He said it in a completely matter-of-fact tone, as if everyone travelled in helicopters all the time. She took a steadying breath, determined not to gawp as if she were impressed. 'Won't your wife find it a bit dull while you're away?' she queried with casual interest.

'No, lady,' he informed her in a sardonic drawl. 'I'm not married.'

His tone rankled with Ros. As if she cared whether he was married or not! She risked another sideways glance at him. He had turned down the collar of his coat, and she could see his face properly.

It was a strikingly handsome face, with strongly carved cheekbones and a faintly aquiline nose. His hair had dried a bit, but it was still almost black, cut short and receding slightly over his temples—but that served only to emphasise the classical symmetry of the bone structure. There was definitely arrogance in the firm line of his mouth, but there was an unmistakable hint of sensuality, too. She couldn't see his eyes, but she was aware that they were watching her steadily.

An odd little frisson of heat shimmered down her spine, and she snatched her gaze away again self-consciously. The last thing she wanted was for this stranger to think he was having some effect on her. She had learned long ago to be wary of good-looking men—learned the hard way.

She had no illusions about her own lack of beauty. She had the sort of face that people usually described as 'interesting', for want of a better word; none of her features seemed quite to fit—her nose was too long, her mouth too wide. And at school they used to call her 'Olive Oyl' because she was so tall and skinny.

But she didn't mind, not any more. She had come to terms with it, and now she had better things to do than worry about what people thought of her. Shaking off the momentary agitation, she enquired politely, 'Are you warm enough now?'

'Fine, thank you.' To her relief, he had stopped looking at her, and relaxed back in his seat. 'I reckon you saved my life. I thought I was going freeze to death out there.'

She laughed, relaxing a little too. 'That would have caused a stir,' she remarked audaciously. 'Mind you, you've created quite a stir already. Everyone's been *dying* to know who'd bought the Priory. It's been odds on in the bar at the White Hart that it was going to be turned into a health farm.'

'Heaven forbid!'

'Or else that it had been bought by one of those weirdo religious set-ups.' She shot him an anxious look. 'You aren't, are you?'

He burst out laughing. 'No, I am not!'

'Only it was all so mysterious,' she explained. 'Why did you keep it such a secret?'

'I like to guard my privacy.'

She nodded—that was something she could understand. 'Have you actually *seen* the house yet?' she asked him.

'No—only a batch of photographs. Quite a ruin, by the look of it. But I understand the builders have made good headway with the renovations. I don't think I'll have to rough it too much.'

'You're not going to spoil it, are you?' she enquired wistfully.

'Not at all, I hope.' He didn't seem to mind her intrusive questioning. 'I'm aiming to restore most of it as authentically as possible—it's had some real bad alterations done to it over the years. But I shall be putting in a few modern conveniences, too—I'm afraid us Yanks are too used to our creature comforts to do without,' he added, an inflection of sardonic humour in his voice. 'I've got to have central heating.'

'Central heating!' Ros sighed with envy, thinking of her own draughty old cottage.

'Is that permitted?' he requested teasingly.

'Oh, I think so.' She slanted him a quick smile. He smiled back, and her heart lurched. His smile had an almost irresistible charm, and in the confined space of the car she was suddenly overpoweringly aware of his physical presence. She swallowed hard, struggling to hide her reaction from him, but she could sense that he was still watching her, and the air between them seemed to crackle with electricity.

He seemed to sense her nervousness at once. 'What's up?' he enquired, a trace of amusement in his voice, as if he was perfectly well aware that he was the cause of her tension.

'N... nothing,' she managed to say. 'I... By the way, we haven't introduced ourselves yet, have we? If we're going to be near neighbours, I can't go on calling you "you".'

'I guess not,' he conceded, an odd quirk of humour in his voice. 'Well, my friends call me Griff.'

Griff—yes, it suited him, she decided, flickering a quick, wary glance in his direction. It had a hard, uncompromising ring to it—she could well imagine that whatever line of business he was in, he could be a tough customer to deal with.

'My name's Ros,' she told him. 'Actually it's Rosalind—my father chose it, but I hate it.'

He laughed softly. 'Why? It's a very pretty name.'

'"Thus Rosalind of many parts by heavenly synod was devis'd"? I don't think that's really me, do you?'

'"Sweetest nut hath sourest rind",' he quoted in return.

She flashed him a look of astonishment. 'You know Shakespeare?'

'We aren't entirely without culture in LA.'

'Oh, I didn't mean... I hope you didn't think...'

He laughed again. 'Not at all. It's all the sun, sea and surf propaganda we put out.'

Rather to her surprise, she found that she was beginning to like him. He had an easy sort of charm... Careful, Rosalind, she reminded herself sharply. You're not a kid any more—you can't claim naïveté as an excuse now. Ten years ago... she had certainly been naïve then!

Maybe if her mother had been alive... but she had died when Ros was only twelve. And her father had been completely out of touch with the modern world.

He had been a highly respected academic, living more in the sixteenth century than the twentieth. He had doted on his only child, in his own rather vague way, but he just hadn't been equipped to prepare her for real life.

At seventeen, she had been painfully coming to terms with the fact that there was little about her that would attract the opposite sex. So, when Stuart Cooper had suddenly started paying her a flattering degree of attention, it had turned her head. She had had a crush on him for ages—all the girls in her sixth-form class had.

She had been easy prey. He had promised her the moon, and she had believed him. It hadn't seemed the least bit wrong or sordid, making love on warm summer evenings, up on the heather-clad moors. And he had listened with seeming interest to her chatter, entering into her vivid fantasy-world—she had been the red-haired Queen Elizabeth the First, he her secret lover, my Noble Lord Essex.

She had been so happy—until that awful night of the harvest festival dance in the church hall. Stuart had completely ignored her, dancing the whole evening with Thea McKenzie. The other boys had started sniggering at her, and one of them had jeered, 'Hey, Queen Elizabeth,' mocking her with an old-fashioned bow—and one of the others had added with a spiteful laugh, '*She* couldn't be Queen Elizabeth. Queen Elizabeth was a virgin.'

She had run all the way home, sick to her stomach. Suddenly she had understood—he had never really been in love with her, he had only been using her, and boasting about her to his mates. She was so upset, she couldn't even face going back to school, knowing that they would all be gossiping about her. Her father, anxious and uncomprehending, had let her make her own choice, even though it had meant forfeiting her place at university.

Ten years ago—but the memory still lingered, like a bad taste in her mouth. But there was no point dwelling on it now. Resolutely she drew her mind back to the present. 'We should be there soon,' she told him. 'I warn you, one blink and you've missed it. There are three shops, a church, and the pub—where ladies are barely tolerated except on Saturday evenings. Mind you, I think you'll feel quite at home,' she added audaciously.

'Oh?'

'Yes.' Her eyes danced as she glanced across at him. 'I've never met such a bunch of male chauvinist pigs!'

'What makes you think I'm a male chauvinist pig?'

'Aren't you?'

'Oh, I wouldn't say so,' he drawled provocatively. 'I just think a woman should know her place.'

'Chained to the kitchen sink, I suppose?'

'Not to the kitchen sink, no,' he returned softly, the mocking note in his voice telling her exactly what he meant.

Ros felt herself blushing furiously, and was glad of the darkness to hide the rush of panic that had seized her. She had never met a man quite like this before, and she felt herself completely out of her depth. Her pulse was beating at an alarming rate. A memory echoed down the years—of the time Stuart Cooper had first smiled at her. It was a warning—look where *that* had led!

Griff was still looking at her. 'What lovely hair you have,' he murmured. 'It's the most incredible colour I've ever seen.' He put up his hand, and coiled a finger into one long corkscrew curl.

'Don't!' She jerked her head away sharply.

'What's wrong?' he asked, startled by the venom in her tone.

'Nothing, just . . . I don't like people touching me,' she snapped in agitation.

At once he sat back in his seat. 'Hey, lady, cool down,' he drawled, a cutting edge of sarcasm in his voice. 'I only touched your hair. I didn't try to rape you.'

Her hands were gripping the wheel so tightly, it was making them ache. She knew she had over-reacted, and now she felt foolish. A long and embarrassing silence stretched between them, as she searched for something to say, regretting the loss of the friendly conversation that had sprung up between them.

'Well, we're there,' she managed at last. 'Look, you can see the lights over there ahead of us. The Priory's up on the hill—to the left, just beyond the village.'

'You live around here yourself?' he asked.

'Just this side of the river.'

'It's very kind of you to go out of your way,' he said, and this time there was no trace of mockery in his voice.

She smiled. 'Not at all. It only takes a minute in the car.'

It had stopped snowing, and the moon had found a tear in the clouds. Its silver light bathed the whole valley. On each side of the road the wild fells lay beneath a thick white blanket, cut into rough squares by the black lines of the dry-stone walls that ran for miles across the moors.

They passed her small cottage, standing all alone behind its long front garden. A few hundred yards further on there was a hump-backed bridge across a fast-flowing river, and then the main street of the village, sloping steeply up to the square-towered church.

The dark grit-stone houses lay well back from the road behind grassy banks now obliterated by snow. Warm lights glowed in most of the windows—Ros could have told Griff the names of every occupant, the names of their children and their aunts and uncles, and probably what their opinions would be on most important topics.

She slanted another swift glance towards him. What would he make of this close-knit community—and what would they make of him? They did not easily accept strangers—had he taken that into account when he had chosen to come and live in this remote place? It was rather an odd thing to do, to leave his home and come half-way round the world to a tiny village that he had never even seen. What had driven him to it?

Where the road forked in front of the church, there were the three shops she had told him about, and the pub. The fork to the right led to a couple of farms, while to the left lay the road that climbed towards the heights of Buckden Pike. A mile or so along that road was the Priory.

Once it had had massive iron gates, but they had been taken away during the war to be melted down for tanks. It was a beautiful old house. Built of the same hard grey stone as the houses in the village, it was a jumble of mediaeval architecture dating from the twelfth century, much of it now covered with ivy. The narrow lancet windows were heavily leaded, and the massive oak door was set in an imposing vaulted stone porch. One wing was still caged in scaffolding, but above the porch a welcoming light showed in the quatrefoil window.

The drive lay under a virgin blanket of snow, six inches deep. The tyres crunched over it as she drew the car to a halt. 'Well, this is it,' she remarked brightly. 'What do you think of it?'

He studied the building in thoughtful silence for a few moments. 'It sure looks old,' he mused.

'It is—up to eight hundred years old, parts of it.'

'That's old!' He slanted her one of those danger-ously attractive smiles. 'Can I offer you a coffee?'

She hesitated, not sure what she was supposed to read into that invitation. 'No, I . . . Thank you, but I've had a long drive from London,' she managed to say, hoping her voice didn't betray her sudden agi-tation. 'I'd better be getting home.'

'OK.' He didn't seem at all offended by her refusal. 'Well, maybe we can take a rain-check on that?'

'Yes, of course.'

He climbed out of the car, picking up his bag from the back seat, and then turned and offered her his hand. Automatically she placed hers in it. But he didn't shake it, as she had expected. Instead he raised it to his lips, woolly glove and all, in a gesture of mocking gallantry. And now she could see his eyes for the first time, lit by the courtesy-light in the car. They were very dark eyes, dark as sin, strangely mesmerising. She felt her heartbeat accelerate alarmingly as she gazed into their fathomless depths.

'*Adieu*, fair Rosalind,' he murmured softly.

The spell was broken as he pushed the car door shut and the courtesy-light switched itself off. Ros blinked in the darkness, almost gasping for breath. Quickly she snatched at first gear, and the tyres slithered in the snow as she spun the steering-wheel a little too sharply.

Her own cottage was dark and very cold. As soon as she pushed open the front door, a sinuous furry body came and wrapped itself around her ankles. She stooped and picked up the cat, and cuddled her in her arms. 'Hello, Cinders,' she murmured. 'You poor thing—it's freezing in here. But I'm not going to bother lighting the fire now—let's just have a cup of tea and go straight to bed, eh?'

The cat purred her agreement, stretching her claws and yawning delicately as Ros carried her through to the kitchen. She kept her coat on while she put the kettle on. Central heating . . . Maybe now that she was starting to make quite a bit of money from her books, she could afford to think about a few modern conveniences herself.

She had lived in Heather Cottage all her life. Some people might have thought it a lonely existence, but she preferred it this way. Her childhood had been very happy, even after her mother had died. She had loved nothing better than to go for long, rambling walks over the moors with her father, or to sit in front of the fire on long winter evenings while he spun her tales of history—stories of the bold seafaring adventurers who had sailed the Spanish Main, fascinating intrigues of the plots behind the Jacobite Rebellion.

But her father had been quite old, and he had suffered a series of strokes—the first not long after those fateful events that had led to her leaving school. She had nursed him for seven years, as he had become increasingly frail, content to live almost like a hermit, her companions those exciting characters of the sixteenth and seventeenth centuries that he had so vividly brought to life for her.

When he had died, three years ago, some of her friends had tried to persuade her to sell the cottage, maybe move to York, or even London. But she hadn't wanted to go. By then she had written her first book, and it had been accepted by a publisher.

She liked being on her own, doing what she wanted when she wanted. If she was absorbed in her writing, sometimes she would sit over her word-processor all night and then not get out of bed until the afternoon; another day she would be up at six and go for a long walk over the moors. Most of the villagers thought her slightly cranky, but she didn't mind that. She could imagine herself living there in fifty years' time, an eccentric old spinster with her black witch's cat.

'I expect you'd like a drop of milk, wouldn't you, Cinders?' she suggested as she poured her tea. Once again the cat made her agreement plain. 'You know, you ought to bring me luck,' she mused as she watched her lapping her milk. 'Oh, I know my books are doing well—I'm not complaining. But just now and then, I wish I could be a pretty numbskull instead. Do you think I might have a fairy godmother somewhere, who could turn me into a beautiful princess?'

The cat regarded her in mild astonishment, and she laughed wryly at herself. 'Oh, what am I talking about? I'm going soft in the head. Come on, let's go to bed.'

CHAPTER TWO

Ros opened her eyes as the cold morning sunlight filtered through the curtains. Shadows of her dreams had chased her into the waking world, but with a determined effort she put all thoughts of the new owner of the Priory out of her mind. Shivering in the frosty air, she darted into the bathroom for a quick wash, and then, pulling on some warm clothes, hurried downstairs to light a fire in the big stone fireplace in the sitting-room.

She made herself some breakfast, and then went to have a look outside. It had snowed quite heavily during the night, and the wind had drifted the snow up against the front door, so that as she opened it she was faced with a three-foot-high wall of snow. She was going to have to dig herself out. With a sigh, she went to search in the glory-hole cupboard under the stairs for a shovel.

It took about half an hour to clear a path to the gate. By the time she had finished she was hot and flushed. She was leaning on her shovel, panting for breath, when suddenly a sardonic voice behind her made her spin round. 'Good morning. You look as if you've been working hard.'

'Oh!' Damn, why did he have to come along *now*, when her face was like a beetroot and her hair all over the place? He was getting out of a sleek silver-grey XJS—slight damage to the front bumper suggested it was the car he had run off the road last night. 'You ... you managed to get it dug out, then?' she remarked, her voice sounding oddly strained to her own ears.

'Yes, thanks. I was lucky—one of the local farmers came along with his tractor, and helped me haul it out. Once I've got the bumper straightened out, it'll be none the worse for wear.'

'Good.'

He surveyed the cottage with interest. 'Nice place you've got here,' he remarked, smiling that much-too-attractive smile. Ros felt her heart-rate climb. 'Is it as old as the Priory?'

'Oh, nowhere near—it's only about two or three hundred years old. I'm afraid it's not in a very good state of repair, either,' she added, suddenly embarrassed by the loose slates and peeling window-frames.

'I can see that.'

'It isn't easy to get workmen to come out here,' she explained defensively. 'Anyway, when the summer comes I'll probably give it a lick of paint myself. I meant to do it last summer, but I was very busy, and I forgot.'

'Couldn't you get one of the men from the village to come up and give you a hand?' he suggested.

'Oh, they probably would, if I asked them,' she confessed. 'But I don't like to—I don't want to be beholden to anyone.' She chose not to add that she didn't want to add fuel to their conviction that a woman couldn't manage alone. She might have guessed that Griff would take a similar line.

'Do you live here all on your own?' he enquired.

'Of course,' she responded, tilting her chin at a proud angle.

He lifted one enquiring eyebrow. 'Why "of course"?'

'Well, who did you think I lived with?' she countered defensively.

'A husband would have been the obvious assumption.'

She felt herself blushing. 'I'm not married,' she answered with a certain amount of constraint. Now he was going to think that she was a frustrated spinster who was going to fall in love with the first passable man who was kind to her. Suddenly all she wanted to do was escape. 'Well, thank you for dropping by,' she managed to say. 'I'm glad your car's not badly damaged. I'll see you around.' She smiled with a confidence she didn't feel, and turned back towards the front door.

'Hey, Ros—hold it' he called after her. She kept walking, pretending she hadn't heard, but he wasn't fooled. 'Suit yourself,' he drawled, a mocking edge of sarcasm in his voice. 'I was just going to point out that there's a whole lot of snow that looks about ready to slide down on to that lean-to there.' He shrugged his wide shoulders, and turned back to his car. 'Now, if it can take the weight, that's fine,' he added, his tone implying that it was a matter of profound indifference to him. 'But I'd have thought it would be a good idea to knock it down on to the path.'

'Oh!' She hurried back out to look. 'Oh, my goodness—yes, you're right—and my car's in there. I'd better climb up.'

'Here, I'll do it for you,' he offered, relenting and holding his hand out for the shovel.

'No, it's OK, I can manage,' she assured him quickly. 'Besides, it wouldn't take your weight.'

'Be careful, then. Where's your ladder?'

'I haven't got one. It's easy enough to get up—see, if I put my foot on this window-sill, and go up the drain-pipe...' She matched the action to the words, scrambling up nimbly and placing her feet carefully so that the strong joists beneath the flimsy bitumen roof-covering would hold her weight. 'Pass me the shovel.'

He handed it up to her with a grin. 'Well, you managed that OK,' he commented.

'Of course. Get out of the way now, or you'll get a snow-shower.' He stood back, and she began to swing at the snow on the roof with the shovel, knocking it safely down on to the path below. It was only when she had finished that she realised that it wasn't going to be as easy to get down as it had been to get up. She peered gingerly over the edge, her first foot-hold tantalisingly out of reach.

He stood with folded arms, watching her with amusement. 'I thought you could manage,' he taunted.

'Oh, don't be horrid,' she wailed in distress. 'Come and help me.'

He strolled over and stood beneath her. 'Jump,' he invited, holding out his arms.

Ros felt a wave of heat course through her body. She hesitated, staring down at the ground. The roof of the lean-to wasn't very high, but from up on top of it, it looked a very long way down. She really didn't have any choice but to let him catch her.

'Come on,' he prompted, a provocative gleam in his dark eyes. 'You'll be quite safe.'

She jumped.

He caught her in his strong arms, barely moving as her weight fell against him. He set her on her feet, but he didn't immediately let her go. 'There. That wasn't so bad, was it?' he taunted gently.

She stared up at him, hoping he would think her breathlessness was entirely due to her exertions. 'Th...thank you,' she stammered unsteadily.

'My pleasure,' he drawled, turning on that devastating smile. 'So—now we're quits. You rescued me from spending all night at the side of the road, and I rescued you from spending all day on the garage roof.'

'Yes.' She wasn't sure what to do, afraid of making a fool of herself by misinterpreting what might be no more than a friendly hug, but aware that if he held her much longer she was going to make a fool of herself anyway. 'Well, I...if you'll excuse me...' she mumbled, trying to ease herself out of his arms.

He laughed—a low, husky laugh that made her shiver with heat. 'What's wrong?' he taunted. 'Anyone would think you had some reason to be afraid of me. You're shaking like a leaf.'

'I...I told you, I don't like being touched.'

A flicker of annoyance crossed his face, and the smile went from his eyes, leaving them hard and cold. 'Pardon me, lady,' he drawled mockingly, letting her go abruptly. 'I'll see you around.'

'Yes. Of... of course. Thank you for your help.' She could feel herself starting to blush, and turned away quickly, running into the house and slamming the door behind her. She leaned against it, closing her eyes. Dammit, why had she behaved in that stupid fashion? He must be thinking she was the village idiot!

It didn't snow any more for the next couple of days, but it stayed very cold. Ros found that the new book wasn't going very well. For some reason, my Noble Lord Essex, cynical and scheming hero of the Elizabethan age, had started to speak with an American accent. She was having no trouble visualising him—tall, dark and extremely attractive, with a hint of that suave confidence of maturity... perhaps his hair should be starting to recede just a little over his temples?

'Damn!' She glared at the screen of the word-processor, cross with herself for letting her mind wander. Impatiently she erased the last couple of paragraphs she had written, and then sat staring blankly at the little green cursor as it flashed in irritating expectation, taunting her to think of the next word.

'Oh, damn you!' she shouted at it, switching off the power and consigning three hours' work to oblivion. If only it were possible to erase her own memory so easily, at the flick of a switch. She pulled the dust-cover over the monitor, and strolled over to the window.

The sun was shining, sparkling on the snow. Above the village, a dozen children were playing with make-shift toboggans on the slope. Beyond, she could just see the long roof of the Priory, with its crenellated parapet and twisted sugar-cane chimneys. She stood for a long time, just gazing at it, her mind drifting aimlessly.

The buzz of the telephone startled her out of her reverie. She hesitated, staring at it blankly. Surely it couldn't be... She snatched up the receiver with a breathless 'Hello?'

'Ros? Hi, it's me. How was London? Did you have a good time?'

She let go her breath in a sigh of relief. She should have guessed it would be Annie—who else would be ringing her on a Friday afternoon? 'Yes, thanks, it wasn't bad. How's the baby?'

'Beginning to kick,' Annie announced complacently. 'Paul says it's much too soon, but he's never been pregnant. Lucy asked me this morning if I could take him out of my tummy so she could see him, and then put him back!'

Ros laughed. Annie had been her best friend ever since they were at school. She was happily married now to Paul Osbourne, the local doctor, and the proud mother of two children, with a third on the way.

'Anyway,' Annie went on, 'I'm ringing up to tell you that you're coming to dinner tomorrow night.'

'Am I?'

'Yes. Eight o'clock. And get out your glad rags, it's going to be posh.'

'I haven't got anything posh,' Ros protested, with little hope of escaping the invitation.

'Yes, you have. What about that nice greeny-blue thing you wore to Thea's party?'

'Annie, that's the *only* posh frock I've got—and I've worn it to every party since the Christmas before last.'

'Well, that's your fault. You could easily afford to buy yourself some nice things now. In fact, you ought to—I'm sick of seeing you in jeans.'

It was impossible to take offence at Annie's blunt manner. Ros laughed again. 'All right, you win,'. she conceded with resignation. 'I'll come, as posh as you like. Who else will be there?'

'Oh, just the usual crowd.'

Ros knew Annie's voice too well to miss the note of suppressed excitement in it. Her heart sank. It would be typical of Annie to be the first to issue an invitation to the fascinating new owner of the Priory. 'Oh?' she enquired drily. 'Glad rags just for the usual crowd?'

Annie giggled. 'Just be here,' she insisted. ''Bye.' She put the phone down before Ros could protest.

The next day was a complete non-starter so far as work was concerned. From the moment Ros opened her eyes, she was thinking of the evening ahead. Much as she chided herself for her idiocy, she just couldn't concentrate. After several false starts she gave it up as a bad job, and threw her nervous energy instead into vigorously spring-cleaning the kitchen.

She worked hard all day, and by the time she had finished she was glad to sink into a warm, relaxing bath. She swirled in a lavish amount of oil, and then lay back in the green foam and closed her eyes, letting the water lap soothingly over her body.

There was absolutely no doubt in her mind that Griff was going to be at Annie's tonight. Well, at least there would be several other women there, so he probably wouldn't even notice her. But, even so, she found herself remembering that brief moment when he had held her in his arms, the mesmerising glint in those dark eyes, and unconsciously she let her hands slide down over her warm, slippery skin, caressing the curves of her body as her mind drifted undisciplined into a realm of pure fantasy...

She woke with a start, to find that the bath water was cold. She jumped out quickly, and towelled herself briskly dry. It was already nearly eight o'clock. She had been thinking of trying to put her hair up, but she didn't have time now, so she just brushed it and left it loose in a mass of curls around her shoulders. A touch of dark blue mascara brought out the blue-grey of her eyes, but that was the only make-up she wore.

Hurriedly dashing herself with eau-de-Cologne, she scrambled into her dress, and cast a quick glance at her reflection in the mirror. She couldn't help feeling just a little bit pleased with her appearance—it was a pretty dress. She had bought it in a wild fit of extravagance with her very first big royalties cheque. Cobweb-soft handkerchiefs of blue-green silk drifted over her shoulders and in deep pointed layers to her knees. It flattered her colouring, and lent a certain gracefulness to her tall figure.

But she didn't have time to stand here admiring herself. Quickly she slipped her feet into her shoes, and ran downstairs. The only coat she had was that old duffel coat—now that she was starting to make some money from her books, she really ought to buy herself something decent. Maybe she ought to think about getting a new car, too, instead of the rattly old banger she had inherited from her father.

Annie lived in a big detached house in the centre of the village, opposite the church. Several cars were parked in the road outside—she guessed that she would be the last to arrive. She parked at the end of the row, and sat for a moment, trying to screw up her courage. They were all there, the usual crowd, just as she had expected.

She could see Thea McKenzie's white Porsche—Thea, who had had such a field-day gossiping about her all those years ago, and then set tongues wagging and fingers counting by the speed with which she had married Stuart Cooper herself, and produced his son and heir.

The marriage had lasted only six years, and her second less than that. Now she was on the prowl again—she had her eye on Annie's brother-in-law Tom. Ros smiled in ironic amusement as she spotted Tom's blue BMW. Thea was going to have a difficult decision to make—especially if Tom had brought his pretty sister, Chrissie. Should she stick to Tom, or should she compete with the younger girl for Griff's attention?

He was there—the sleek silver-grey Jaguar was parked by the kerb a little way in front of Tom's car. Well, at least forewarned was fore-armed, she thought wryly. Taking a deep, steadying breath, she climbed out of the car and walked up to the front door.

Light and music spilled into the night as Annie opened the door, excitement written all over her face.

"I thought you were never coming!' she whispered, drawing her into the hall.

'I'm sorry. I dozed off in the bath, and didn't realise it was getting so late.'

'Dozed off? Aren't you the cool one?' teased Annie, hanging Ros's duffel coat up in the hall right next to Thea's expensive fox-fur jacket. 'Just *wait* till you see who I've got to introduce to you!'

There were several people gathered in Annie's large sitting-room, but Ros saw only one. He was sitting back, totally relaxed, on one of the big farmhouse-style settees, looking devastatingly attractive in a dark green velvet jacket. Chrissie Osbourne had established herself at his side, and was gazing up at him in ingenuous admiration. Thea was seated opposite him, her long legs elegantly crossed, her slim, scarlet-tipped fingers holding a cigarette.

The stereo was playing one of her all-time favourite albums, the smokily seductive male voice filling the room. Ros hesitated, her heart slowing to a halt. That arrogant tilt of the head, that faintly mocking smile... How on earth had she failed to recognise him? She had had his picture on her bedroom wall all through her teens—she still played his records more than any others she owned.

Jordan Griffin. Ex-lead-singer of one of the biggest American rock-music bands ever. Since he'd retired— oh, it must be four or five years ago now since the band had gone their separate ways—he'd turned to managing other people, being responsible for the careers of several massively successful artists.

Annie pushed her forward as she stood rooted to the spot. 'Well, she's here at last. Jordan, I want you

to meet my best friend, Rosalind Hammond. Go on,'
she hissed at Ros, 'say hello. He won't bite.'

He rose to his feet, that mocking smile curving his
sensuous mouth as he let his eyes drift lazily down
over her body. 'Ros and I have already met,' he
drawled, a trace of sardonic amusement in his voice.

She felt a tinge of pink creep up over her cheeks.
'I . . . I'm sorry,' she stammered breathlessly. 'I didn't
recognise you.'

'So I guessed.'

Across the room, Thea laughed spitefully. 'Ah,
that's our Rosalind,' she put in. 'Not really interested
in modern music, are you, darling? She's our local
blue-stocking you know, Jordan.'

'Really?' He had detected that Thea was jealous of
the momentary diversion of his attention away from
herself, and his eyes glinted with malignant
amusement. 'What sort of music do you prefer, then,
Ros?' he enquired. His tone was pleasant, friendly,
but she knew that he was playing a game, deliberately
seeking to provoke Thea.

'Good music,' she retorted, instilling a cool note of
sarcasm into her voice.

'Oh? Mozart, Beethoven, that sort of thing?'

'More or less.'

The atmosphere in the room was fairly crackling
with electricity. It felt as though World War Three
were going to break out at any minute. Annie stepped
quickly into the silence, putting on her best hostess
voice. 'Well, now that everyone's here, why don't we
go into the dining-room?' she suggested, glancing
anxiously from one to another to see how they would
respond.

'Great,' agreed her husband, coming quickly to her support. 'I'll promise you one thing, Jordan—you won't be disappointed in my wife's cooking.'

Griff smiled. 'I'm looking forward to it. By the way, my friends call me Griff,' he added, flickering an amused glance towards Ros.

'Of course. You know, I've been thinking—I bet there's some cousins of yours still living over in Hamblethorpe. Brian Griffin—his grandfather, used to work on Arnold Fowler's farm.'

As the others moved through the open-plan archway into the dining-room, Ros followed Annie into the kitchen to see if she could help with the dinner. 'You *are* a dark horse,' her friend remarked, slanting her a teasing glance. 'Why didn't you tell me you'd met him?'

Ros smiled wryly. 'I really *hadn't* recognised him,' she confessed. 'It was dark. It happened the other night—the night it snowed. His car had gone off the road, and I gave him a lift, that's all.' She conveniently forgot the rest of the story. 'Anyway, you can talk!' she added, turning the conversation before Annie could probe further. 'Trust you to be the first to invite him to dinner!'

'It wasn't me, it was Paul,' Annie confided. 'Would you believe it, he actually *knows* him, and he never even told me! Remember he worked for a year in Central America when he first qualified? He met him then. Apparently he gives a lot of money to hospitals and things in the poor areas.'

'I never knew that,' remarked Ros.

'No—he doesn't like any publicity about it. Anyway, yesterday morning one of the men working on his house had an accident—cut his hand really badly—and Griff brought him down to the surgery himself. Well, of course, they got nattering, and it was only natural for Paul to invite him to dinner.' She sighed, and rolled her eyes expressively. 'Just think, ten years ago, if this had happened, we'd have been like jelly now! In fact, I am a bit sort of wobbly round the edges. He's absolutely gorgeous, isn't he? I think he's even better-looking now than he was then.'

'Annie! And you a married woman!' Ros chided her teasingly.

Annie giggled. 'I know. But there's no harm in *looking*, is there?'

'I do think it was a bit mean of you, inviting both Thea *and* Chrissie,' Ros commented, glancing into the softly lit dining-room where the two rivals were jockeying for the prime places close to him at the dinner-table. 'The poor man's in danger of being eaten alive.'

'Poor man, indeed! You should have seen him, playing them off against each other—I had to run away to the kitchen, or I wouldn't have been able to keep my face straight.'

'He does seem to be enjoying it,' confessed Ros, hoping Annie wouldn't notice the slightly wistful note in her voice.

'I think they're both making complete idiots of themselves,' her friend declared roundly. 'As if he's going to be interested in either of them. Look at all those really fabulous women he's been out with! He's just amusing himself, and more fool them if they take him seriously.'

'I suppose you're right,' conceded Ros thought-fully. And even more fool me, she chided herself. Now she had even more reason to know that he was never in a million years going to be interested in her. But it didn't help—the man in the flesh exerted a tug of attraction a hundred times more powerful than the unreachable idol she had adored in her teens.

'Anyway, come on. We'd better be taking this stuff in,' said Annie, oblivious of her friend's train of thought. 'Can you carry this pâté for me?'

To her relief, Ros was able to sit a safe distance away from Griff. He was on Paul Osbourne's right at the other end of the table. Chrissie had artlessly plopped herself down beside him and started a bright conversation with Nigel, Paul's partner and always an obliging 'spare man' at Annie's dinner parties. Thea, cheated of the chance to be next to Griff, had ruthlessly manoeuvred so that she could take the seat opposite him, and found that it was just as easy to flirt with him across the table.

Tom Osbourne grinned at Ros in his usual friendly way as he rose to help her to a seat. 'Hi. You're looking very nice tonight,' he complimented her lightly.

She returned him a warm smile. Tom had always been nice to her, even though he had been one of Stuart Cooper's crowd in the old days.

'So, are you madly in love with our new neighbour, too?' he asked her in a wry tone.

She shook her head. 'I gave up being in love with pop stars when I was sixteen,' she responded casually. 'Besides, he seems to have his hands full at the moment.'

From beneath her lashes, she watched the scene that was developing at the other end of the table. The competition between the two women was growing increasingly sharp, and the arrogance in Griff's smile was unmistakable as he absorbed their unabashed adoration.

How on earth had she failed to recognise him? His hair was much shorter now, of course, but the features were exactly those that had brooded from the covers of a dozen top-selling albums. Of course, she had never expected him to turn up in Arnby Bridge.

His eyes flickered in her direction, and immediately she turned all her attention to Tom. 'Annie was telling me you might be made a partner soon,' she remarked quietly. Tom worked for a local firm of solicitors.

'That's right. George is retiring this summer, so I might be taking his place.'

'Well done,' she flattered, her eyes dancing merrily.

'It's a step in the right direction. Speaking of which, when are you going to sell me that cottage of yours?'

She laughed, shaking her head. 'I'm not ready to sell yet, Tom.'

'Well, if ever you change your mind . . .'

'You'll be the first to know,' she promised.

They chatted easily as they did justice to the excellent dinner that Annie had set before them, a little withdrawn from the acid rivalry that was developing at the other end of the table. The two girls were letting themselves be drawn into a heated competition for Griff's attention, apparently unaware of the glint of cynical amusement in those dark eyes as he subtly manipulated them both.

'But you're going to find it *so* different over here,' Thea was telling him. 'It's like another planet.'

'Oh?' One satanic eyebrow was raised a fraction of an inch. 'I don't think Ros would agree with you—would you, Ros?'

Suddenly she was aware that everyone was watching her, and she looked up, uncertain. He was regarding her with that mocking gaze, and in that moment she felt as though she hated him. 'I beg your pardon?' she queried in glacial accents.

'Didn't you say that I'd feel very much at home—among all the male chauvinist pigs?' he taunted.

She hesitated, unable to think of a suitable retort.

Chrissie gurgled with laughter. 'Oh, Ros! What a thing to say!' she protested. 'I'm sure Griff isn't like that at all!' She swept him a lingering gaze from beneath her silky lashes.

'Oh, all this feminist talk is such a lot of nonsense,' put in Thea, her voice a velvet purr. 'I like a man who knows he's the boss.'

Coming from Thea, that was such a preposterous statement that Ros couldn't quite suppress the smile that twitched her lips.

The other woman's eyes sparked with anger. 'But then, you wouldn't really know about that, would you, Ros?' she sneered spitefully. 'You couldn't even hang on to Stuart.'

'Nor could you,' Chrissie reminded everyone with malicious triumph.

'But at least he married me,' flashed Thea haughtily.

Ros could feel her cheeks flame scarlet with humiliation, painfully aware of Griff's curiosity as he watched the barbed exchange.

Annie, bless her, came to the rescue. 'Well, does everyone want coffee?' she asked brightly. 'Ros, give me a hand, would you?'

'Of course.' With an inward sigh of relief, she began to gather up the debris of the sweet-plates, and made her escape to the kitchen.

CHAPTER THREE

THAT brief moment of unpleasantness soon seemed to be forgotten. They lingered long at the dinner-table over their coffee, until by some unspoken consent they chose to move back into lounge to talk and drink. Thea had latched her arm through Griff's, coaxing him to sit beside her, but Chrissie wasn't going to let her get away with that. She was leaning casually over the back of their settee, engaging his attention in a flirtatious conversation.

From across the room, Ros watched them with covert interest. It was small wonder that he was so arrogant, she reflected wryly. It must always be like that, wherever he went—beautiful women throwing themselves at him. And plain women too, she amended, remembering her own behaviour. It must be very tedious for him.

'Why don't we have some music on?' Thea proposed, determined to reclaim all Griff's attention. She moved with an eye-catching sway across the room to the music centre, and chose a record—one of Griff's. But as she opened the cover he came up behind her, and took it away from her.

'Not that one,' he murmured, bending close to her ear. 'Let's have something different for a change, shall we?'

She swept him a coy glance from beneath her sooty lashes. 'All right—anything you like,' she purred.

One dark eyebrow was raised a fraction of an inch. 'Anything?'

She laughed huskily. 'In the way of music,' she chided—though she didn't sound as if that was what she meant. She picked out another record, and slotted it into the record player. Soft, romantic music filled the room. 'Shall we dance?' she invited him boldly.

He let his gaze drift down over the luscious curves of her body, displayed to perfection by the clinging fit of her black dress. 'Sure,' he agreed, taking her into his arms and holding her intimately close. Over her shoulder, Ros caught a glimpse of that dark, sinful glint in his eyes. She looked away quickly.

Chrissie was quietly fuming. She grabbed her eldest brother's hand, and pulled him to his feet. 'Come on, Paul,' she insisted with a lively laugh. 'Let's give it a whirl.'

'I didn't know we were going to be holding a ball,' he protested, smiling down indulgently at his pretty sister.

'Oh, just a little dancing,' she pouted. 'It won't hurt—the kids are over at Annie's mother's.' She began to move to the music, swaying provocatively for Griff's benefit. Thea was glowering with fury as he watched the performance with every evidence of appreciation.

Tom grinned wryly at Ros. 'Come on then, lass,' he suggested. 'Let's not be the only ones left out, eh?'

Ros understood—he wasn't going to let Thea suspect that he was the least bit bothered by her behaviour. She was more than willing to assist—she had a similar motive herself. Besides, she liked dancing—

a good rhythm could make her forget her usual self-consciousness.

She kept her back turned to Griff as she danced, letting Tom flirt with her outrageously. It didn't take Thea long to notice what was going on—and she didn't like it one little bit. What was sauce for the goose was *definitely* not sauce for the gander in her book. And she had enough sense to realise that, though Griff might indulge her with a brief affair, she was unlikely to get more than that from him—and she wasn't about to let a good catch like Tom Osbourne slip through her fingers. Suddenly Ros found herself being ruthlessly manipulated into a change of partners.

'Oh, Tom! How sweet of you to dance with poor Ros.' Thea was smiling at her, but her eyes glinted maliciously. 'But I'm sure you're just *dying* for a chance to dance with Griff, aren't you, darling? I really mustn't monopolise him all evening.'

She handed him over generously, and Ros found herself in his arms. She held herself stiffly, trying to keep some space between them, remembering all too vividly how it had felt to be so close to him the other morning. He had taken off his white bow-tie and unfastened the top button of his shirt, and inside his collar she could just glimpse a few dark hairs that curled at the base of his throat. Her mouth felt suddenly dry.

'Come on, relax,' he coaxed, his voice warm and persuasive. 'I feel as if I'm dancing with a robot.'

'I'm sorry. I'm not much of a dancer.'

'Oh, I wouldn't say that,' he drawled, a hint of sensual promise in his smile. 'I was watching you just now with Paul's brother. You've a natural rhythm—

when you forget that you don't like to be touched. Or is it just me who provokes that reaction?'

'No... I... it's different when you're dancing,' she temporised, her voice taut with agitation.

'Then relax.' That deep, velvet voice held a seductive quality that was very hard to resist. The warm strength of his arms was melting the ice in her spine, and the faintly musky male smell of his body was drugging her mind. 'That's better,' he murmured, his breath fanning her hair. 'Why are you so nervous all the time? You're like a teenager—no confidence in yourself.'

'I can't help that,' she mumbled against the collar of his jacket.

'But why?' he persisted. 'You're a very attractive woman.'

'Don't!' She almost flinched away from him. 'I know I'm not beautiful, and I don't care. But I hate that sort of stupid attempt at flattery.'

A dark flash of annoyance lit his eyes. 'I'm not flattering you,' he retorted bluntly. 'Of course you're not beautiful—I didn't say you were. You don't need to be—the effect you have on men has got nothing at all to do with having a pretty face.'

She felt her cheeks tinge with pink, and looked away from him quickly. 'I... I don't know what you mean,' she protested thickly.

'No?' He laughed softly. 'I don't believe that. I don't think I can be the only one to sense it—it's like a fire inside you.' His hand slid slowly down her back to mould intimately over the base of her spine, holding her far too close for modesty. Somehow he had woven a spell around her; the way they were moving to the slow, sensuous rhythm of the music . . . it was almost as if they were making love.

She shook her head, trying to ease herself away from him. 'No,' she protested in a strangled whisper. 'I'm not like that . . . At least . . .'

'It's nothing to be ashamed of,' he murmured, those dark eyes weaving a mesmerising spell. 'I don't suppose you can help it.'

She *did* know what he had meant—she had seen it often, that look in men's eyes. It had made her wary, afraid that they had detected that shameful flaw in her character that would make her an easy conquest. So she had rigidly avoided any kind of involvement, and most men had been easy enough to put off.

But this was no ordinary man. This was Jordan Griffin. She couldn't think straight when she was so close to him—she had to get away. 'Excuse me,' she managed to say, resolutely disentangling herself from his arms. 'I . . . I just . . . I won't be a minute.' She hurried from the room, ran upstairs to the bathroom and bolted the door behind her.

She was trembling uncontrollably. What was going on—why was he picking on her like this? He had Thea and Chrissie absolutely falling over themselves to attract his interest—couldn't he be satisfied? Or did he have to prove that he could wind *every* woman around his little finger?

She made herself look at her reflection in the mirror, trying hard to pull herself together. Come off it, Rosalind Hammond, she scolded herself severely. Jordan Griffin isn't going to waste five minutes on you.

That made her feel better, but she really couldn't face going back downstairs. Annie would understand if she slipped quietly away. Quickly she splashed cold water over her flushed cheeks, then opened the bathroom door.

He was standing at the top of the stairs, leaning against the wall, his arms folded across his wide chest, a taunting smile curving his hard mouth.

'Running away?'

She drew in a sharp breath. 'No. Of course not—why should I?'

'Why, indeed?' He took a step towards her, and she backed away. 'Just what are you afraid of, fair Rosalind?' he mocked her in that soft, velvety voice.

'Nothing. I just ... I'm going home now. I've got a lot to do.'

He shook his head. 'Not a very good excuse,' he derided. 'You're far too much of a lady to run out on your best friend's dinner party.'

She tilted her chin up haughtily. 'How would you know?' she countered, her voice betraying her tension.

He laughed, low and huskily, coming closer. '*Aren't* you a lady?' he taunted. 'Now, that could be very interesting.'

She couldn't retreat any further—he had backed her into a corner. 'You ... you don't need me. You've no shortage of entertainment downstairs,' she protested acidly.

He shook his head. 'At the risk of sounding conceited, I find that sort of thing rather boring. I'm much more interested in you. What was all that about at the dinner-table? Who's this Stuart?'

She sought desperately for a way to dodge past him, but she was trapped on the narrow landing. He came slowly towards her, and put his hands against the wall on each side of her shoulders.

'Well? Are you going to tell me?'

She tried to twist away from him. 'Stop it,' she pleaded in a broken whisper. 'Please, leave me alone.'

'Not until you tell me what it was all about.' With one tantalising fingertip he traced a path along her hairline, pushing a wayward strand of curls back from her face. 'I gather he was Thea's first husband.' She nodded dumbly. 'And she stole him from you?'

'Sort of,' she mumbled.

He laughed softly. 'He strikes me as a pretty dumb klutz,' he remarked. 'Have you been carrying a torch for him ever since?'

'Oh, no.' Her smile matched his for cynicism. 'I'm really rather grateful to him—he taught me a lesson about men I've never forgotten.'

'Which is?'

'Never do a thing unless you're prepared to have it announced on the BBC News next day.'

He smiled with unexpected sympathy. 'Is that what he did? Poor Ros—that can't have been very nice in a small town like this.' She blinked at him, astonished by his understanding. 'How old were you?'

'S . . . seventeen.'

'And did he have a lot to tell?'

She lowered her eyes, her cheeks scarlet with humiliation. He drew her unresisting into his arms, holding her head gently against his shoulder. 'And you've been paying for that one mistake ever since?' he murmured softly. 'You little fool—you didn't commit any crime. I guess the flames must have got too hot before you were old enough to know how to control them. That's no reason to let it ruin the rest of your life.'

He laced his fingers into her hair, drawing her head back until she found herself gazing up into those compelling dark eyes. She felt as though her bones were dissolving away. As he bent towards her she could do nothing to defend herself. His mouth brushed lightly over hers, warm and enticing, and her lips parted. The sensuous tip of his tongue swirled languorously over the delicate membranes, finding every sensitive corner.

He was sweeping away all the defences she had so painfully learned to erect, and as his arms wrapped around her she could only surrender, letting him curve her against the hard length of his body in a way that stirred her responses to white heat.

At last he lifted his head and smiled down into her eyes. 'You see? What can be wrong in doing something that comes so naturally?' he cajoled, honey-tongued.

Weakly she tried to struggle free. 'Please . . . let me go,' she whispered.

'Not yet,' he answered, letting his hand rove intimately over her body. 'You've got a lot of wasted time to make up.'

Her head tipped back into the crook of his arm as his long, clever fingers brushed up over the warm swell of her breast. A small sob escaped her lips, and her knees almost gave way beneath her, but he held her close as he caressed her with merciless skill, reducing her to a helpless, quivering wreck.

If it had been any other man... But she couldn't forget who he was. Why should Jordan Griffin want to make love to a ginger-haired scarecrow like her? He was just amusing himself—her reluctance was probably stimulating to a palate jaded by too many easy conquests. A sudden surge of anger rose inside her, and she pushed him away.

'I said, let me go,' she hissed furiously. 'You really think you're God's gift to women, don't you?' In the instant that he stepped back, startled by her reaction, she took the opportunity to slip past him. 'Save your irresistible charm for the likes of Chrissie and Thea,' she spat. 'What sort of fool do you think I am?'

'I haven't quite made up my mind yet,' he retorted, infuriatingly cool.

'Not fool enough to let myself get swept off my feet by the likes of you,' she declared with dignity. 'I told you, I learned my lesson a long time ago. Thank you for fulfilling one of my teenage fantasies—I wish I'd been young enough to appreciate it.'

There was a sardonic edge in his laughter. 'Maybe. But you're not exactly an old maid yet—however hard you try to act the part. It isn't so easy to douse those flames, is it?'

With a flounce she turned her back on him and marched down the stairs. But, as she reached the bottom, Annie came out of the sitting-room. 'Oh, there you—— What are you doing?' she interrupted herself as Ros reached for her coat. 'You're not leaving, are you?'

Ros cast her a bright smile. 'Yes. Sorry, Annie,' she said breathlessly. 'I'm really right in the middle of something at the moment. You know what I'm like.

Sorry to dash away so early. Thanks for the dinner—it was really nice.'

Annie hesitated, looking from her to Griff and back again. 'Is everything all right?' she asked, frowning.

'Of course.' She shrugged herself into her coat. 'Goodnight, Annie. G-goodnight, Griff.'

'Goodnight,' he responded, those dark eyes mocking her cowardice. 'Perhaps we can continue our...discussion...another time?'

Annie's eyes widened as she picked up the powerful undercurrents of tension in the air. 'Goodnight, Ros,' she conceded, following her to the front door, but as they stepped out into the porch she demanded in an insistent whisper, 'What's been going on?'

'Nothing, I told you. What do you mean?' Ros answered, trying for an air of innocence.

'Oh, come on,' countered Annie shrewdly. 'Were you having a row with him or something?'

'Of course not. What could I possibly have to row with him about?'

'I don't know. But the way you ran out on him when you were dancing...'

'I didn't. I just...got a bit annoyed with him. He's a bit too big for his boots—just because he's Jordan Griffin, he thinks every woman he meets is going to swoon at his feet.'

Annie laughed. 'Oh, come off it! He isn't a bit conceited—at least, only when dumbos like Chrissie and Thea are making cow-eyes at him, and you can't blame him for that.'

Ros chuckled with laughter. 'Oh, Annie! You're besotted. And you a respectable married woman!'

'I'm not besotted—I just think he's nice. Fancy him coming to live here in Arnby Bridge! I never even knew he had a family connection. I wonder why he decided to leave California. All that lovely sun—not much of an exchange, is it?' she added wryly, shivering at the cold night air.

'Why don't you ask him?'

'I don't like to pry.'

'Well, that's a first!'

'Ros! Are you trying to make out that I'm nosy?' Annie protested indignantly. 'I mean... Well, I do like to know what's going on, but that's different. Griff's a stranger.'

Ros smiled indulgently at her friend. 'You'll ask him, sooner or later,' she teased. 'Anyway, I'd better be off now—it's freezing out here. Goodnight.'

'Goodnight, Ros. And don't go shutting yourself up for weeks on end with that book, as you did last time. If you do, I'll come and dig you out.'

Ros laughed. 'OK, I'll try not to. 'Bye.'

Annie waved goodbye as she drove away. Ros smiled sadly to herself. She did envy her friend—a loving husband, beautiful children... Sometimes her little cottage seemed such a lonely place. Impatiently she shook her head to dispel the melancholy mood that was threatening to descend on her. It was stupid to dwell on 'might-have-beens'.

She'd probably never been cut out for marriage, anyway—what man would tolerate a wife who could disappear into the sixteenth century for days at a time? And as for babies... if she was in the middle of a chapter, she'd probably forget to feed them, let alone change their nappies. No, it was better the way it was—with only an aloof black cat to worry about.

Next morning the thaw set in, and with it came disaster. It started as a steady drip-drip-drip that Ros heard as she was eating her breakfast. She rushed upstairs, to find the ceiling of her bedroom dripping water in several places.

She almost fell down the stairs in her haste to get to the kitchen, trying to remember where to find the stopcock. She found it after throwing everything out of the cupboard under the sink, but she couldn't turn it off. The dripping from the burst pipes was getting ominously louder and faster by the minute. She tugged and pulled on the tap in desperation, but it wouldn't budge.

In a panic she grabbed as many pans as she could carry, and ran back upstairs. Working as quickly as she could, she put a pan under each drip—only to find more leaks coming through in the next room. Almost sobbing with worry and frustration, she ran downstairs again and hunted for more pans.

In the end she was using everything she could think of to catch the drips, from the washing-up bowl to a Victorian chamber-pot she had been using as a plant-holder. When she thought she'd dealt with all the leaks she ran down to the kitchen to have another go at the tap, but still nothing would move it. Quickly she hunted in the cupboard under the stairs, and found an old tub of grease to rub around the tap to try to free it, but still it obstinately defied all her efforts.

Her hair was falling in her eyes, and she pushed it back impatiently, not even noticing that she was smearing grease on her face. Then it was time to rush back upstairs to check the pots, and she spent the next few minutes frantically emptying the pots into the bath and replacing them before they overflowed.

'Damn, damn, damn!' she muttered to herself over and over. She'd meant to look at the lagging on the pipes during the summer, but she had forgotten all about it. She only had herself to blame for this disaster—they must be leaking in twenty places now.

With a sigh she pulled the ladder down from the loft-hatch, and climbed up to take a look. It was very dusty up there, and she walked into a cobweb that made her jump. The pipes were a mess, the lagging chewed by mice or birds or something. She struggled back down the ladder, and sat on the bottom step to indulge herself with a flood of tears.

The sound of a knock startled her. Heedless of her scruffy appearance, she ran down the stairs and yanked open the front door. Griff stood on the doorstep. His eyebrows shot up in astonishment as he looked down at her, but she didn't even stop to think.

'Oh, thank goodness!' she gasped, grabbing him by the arm and dragging him into the kitchen. 'There,' she said, pointing at the rusting pipe under the sink. 'The stopcock—can you turn it off?'

He looked bemused, but he didn't argue. Quickly he got down on his knees to have a go at the tap. It took both hands, and considerable effort, but at last he did it. At once he turned on the tap at the sink to drain the system, and within a few seconds the dripping upstairs had ceased.

'Phew!' sighed Ros with heartfelt relief, plumping down on a stool. 'Thank you. I thought the whole ceiling would collapse before anyone came.'

'You should keep this tap greased,' he told her, frowning. 'It's rusting up. Is there much damage?'

'The ceilings in a couple of the bedrooms are pretty bad,' she told him.

'Let's have a look.' She led him upstairs to her bedroom, neither of them considering anything but the damage to the old cottage. He surveyed the ceilings with a grave expression. 'It *is* bad,' he agreed. 'You won't be able to use the lights for a couple of days— the whole place could go up in flames.'

'How long do you think it will take to dry out?' she asked.

'It depends on the weather,' he said, glancing out of the window. 'Tuesday, maybe. Let's have a look in the loft.'

'It's filthy up there,' she warned.

'I dare say,' he remarked drily, flicking a glance of mocking amusement over her dishevelled appearance. 'Show me.'

She found a torch, and handed it up to him as he climbed the steps into the loft. He didn't seem to mind the dust, but his face was grim as he came back down the ladder.

'You'll have to get those pipes replaced,' he warned her. 'And you'll have to get the roof done—there are a lot of tiles missing, and the birds have been getting in and out and pecking at the lagging.' Her eyes filled with tears again, and he looked down at her in concern. 'Can't you afford it?' he asked gently.

'It's not that. It's just that it's so difficult to get workmen to come out here, or do a proper job,' she explained as he followed her down to the kitchen. 'I suppose they think . . . when they see it's a woman on her own . . . they can take advantage,' she added reluctantly.

He moved towards her as if to take her in his arms, and at that moment she would have sunk into them gladly—but suddenly she realised what a mess she must look, and a wave of embarrassment swept through her. She pulled away from him, her cheeks flaming scarlet.

'Would you like a coffee?' she managed to ask. But as she put out her hand to pick up the kettle she remembered there was no water. That really was the last straw. She banged her fist on the draining-board in exasperation. The safe little life she had built for herself had been completely overturned in the past few days, and all because of this intrusive man. If it hadn't been for those damned pipes, she would never have let him over her threshold—but now here he was, in her cluttered kitchen, like an invader, leaving her nowhere else to run.

She was conscious that he had come up close behind her. Although he didn't touch her, a charge like static electricity seemed to leap the physical gap between them, and her body quivered as if he had caressed her. But he seemed to sense that her nerves were drawn taut enough to snap, and he made no move to press home his advantage.

'What will you do till you can get the place fixed?' he asked, genuine concern in his voice. 'Have you somewhere you could stay?'

'I could go down to Annie's,' she responded, trying to appear casual as she moved away from him to put the kitchen table between them.

'Ring her up, then,' he suggested. 'I'll take you over there.'

'It's OK—I can manage, thank you,' she protested.

He shook his head. 'You don't look as if you're in a fit state to drive anywhere,' he insisted in a voice that would brook no resistance. 'Come on, don't argue—go and fix it with Annie, and pack yourself a few things.'

She caved in without further dispute—it was so nice to have someone take everything over for her. She went out into the hall, and dialled Annie's number.

Annie was instantly sympathetic. 'Of course you can stay,' she agreed at once. 'Can you manage OK? Shall I come over and pick you up?'

'No, it's all right,' Ros answered quickly. 'I'll be over in about twenty minutes.'

'Right. See you later.'

When she went back into the kitchen, Griff was sitting at the table. He glanced up at her with a smile. 'OK?'

She nodded. 'I . . . thank you very much for your help,' she managed to say. 'I don't know what I'd have done if you hadn't come along.'

He laughed softly. 'I have to admit, it wasn't quite the reception I usually get.'

She felt her cheeks tinge with pink. 'I'm sorry,' she murmured. 'Was there . . . was there something you wanted, by the way?'

Those dark eyes were smiling into hers. 'I came to apologise for last night,' he told her. 'I didn't mean to upset you. I'm afraid characters like your two friends bring out the worst in me.'

She managed a shaky laugh. 'I'd have thought you'd have been used to it by now.'

'I ought to be,' he agreed. 'It made quite a pleasant change to meet someone who didn't know me from Adam.'

His easy charm was making her relax, and she smiled back at him. 'I felt such a fool,' she admitted.

'No, why should you?' he argued. 'I hope my ego never got so big I expected to be recognised by everyone. And besides, if you're not into modern music . . .'

'Oh, that's not strictly true,' she confessed. 'I do like some of it. In fact, I think I've still got a couple of your records somewhere.' As soon as she had said it, she felt herself blushing again. He was going to see right through that—she had tried just a little too hard to be casual. 'Well, I . . . I'll just go and throw a few things into a bag, and . . . oh, I'd better find Cinders.'

'Cinders?'

'My cat. She does tend to wander off.'

Just at that moment the black cat strolled into the kitchen, and after a brief interrogation of Griff's ankles, of which she evidently approved, she lifted her front paws against his knees, padding delicately, her head coquettishly on one side.

'Stop that!' Ros scolded sharply. 'Griff doesn't want you clawing him to pieces.'

He stooped and picked the cat up, tucking her comfortably into the crook of his arm. 'She wouldn't do that,' he asserted, his tone implying that he would know just how to deal with her if necessary. Cinders responded to such high-handed treatment with a sensuous purr.

For one stupid moment, Ros even felt jealous of the cat—there seemed to be a glint of triumph in those slanting green eyes, and something distinctly smug in the way she nestled down in his arms. Impatiently she pulled herself together. 'I won't be a minute,' she promised, and made good her escape.

CHAPTER FOUR

IT TOOK only a few minutes to drive round to Annie's. Unfortunately, Ros had forgotten it was the middle of Paul's morning surgery, and every gossip in the village was there to see them draw up at the kerb. She smiled wryly. 'Oh, dear—this will give them all something to talk about,' she sighed.

He laughed. 'Well, if they've nothing better to do...' He got out of the car, came round to open her door for her, and then went to fetch her bag from the boot.

'Thank you,' she murmured, aware of several interested pairs of eyes watching them. 'And thank you very much for the lift, and for fixing the tap.'

He slanted her a teasing smile. 'Well, that seems a fairly comprehensive list. Sure you haven't forgotten anything?'

An answering twinkle of mirth danced in her eyes. 'No, I don't think so,' she answered, pretending to give the matter serious consideration.

At that moment Annie threw open the front door and, when she saw who had brought her friend, the expression on her face made Ros gurgle with laughter.

'Ros!' She stared from one to the other, a dozen urgent questions barely restrained by a fixed smile. 'What...? Come inside. I'll put the kettle on. Er... how about you, Griff?' she added, ignoring her friend's attempts to signal a discreet protest. 'Would you like a cup of tea?'

'Thank you very much—I don't mind if I do,' he agreed readily.

'What's going on?' Annie hissed to Ros as they walked into the house. 'How come he brought you down?'

'It's a long story,' she whispered back. 'I'll tell you later.'

'Do you know, I had a suspicion—I said as much to Paul last night. He fancies you.'

'Oh, don't be silly,' Ros countered quickly, hoping she wasn't blushing. 'He just . . . We *did* have a bit of a row last night, and he came round to apologise, that's all.'

Annie slanted her a dubious glance. 'Oh, yes? *Just* to apologise?'

'*Just* to apologise,' Ros insisted. 'Go on, I'll make the tea. You can go and make cow-eyes at him.'

'I don't make cow-eyes,' protested Annie indignantly. 'Not at anyone.'

But when, five minutes later, Ros carried the tray of teacups into the sitting-room, it was evident that, if Annie hadn't quite succumbed to Griff's charm, he had fallen completely under the spell of her two small children. He was sitting on the floor with them, playing with the cat.

Annie was watching comfortably from the settee, her needles clicking busily as she knitted one of the unrecognisable little garments she always reproduced endlessly when pregnant—Ros had never yet seen one of her babies wearing any of them.

Griff glanced up as she entered, and smiled. 'Ah, tea! I'm beginning to develop a taste for it already.

The men working on my house always have a pot...mashing? Is that the word?'

Ros nodded, laughing. 'That's right. We'll teach you to speak proper English yet!'

The children scrambled up from the floor, and ran to her, hugging her legs. 'Auntie Ros. Squash! Squash!' lisped four-year-old Lucy imploringly.

'Say please,' her mother reminded her with gentle patience.

Huge blue eyes, fringed by thick silky lashes, gazed meltingly up at Ros. 'Please.'

Ros smiled indulgently. 'All right. Do you want some too, Peter?' The two-year-old nodded his blond head solemnly. 'Sit down and watch Thomas the Tank Engine, then,' she coaxed, setting the tea-tray down on a low table.

'Now, then,' she heard Annie scold as she went back into the kitchen. 'Uncle Griff doesn't want you two climbing all over him.'

Griff laughed with genuine pleasure. 'It's OK,' he assured her. 'They're real nice kids. I never had much to do with kids before.'

'That's a pity,' remarked Annie, in a tone designed to prompt further confidences. Ros poured the squash, all her attention focused on the conversation in the next room. 'You don't have any brothers or sisters, do you?'

'No, I don't. A few of my friends had kids, of course, but I never got to spend much time with them. I guess I was always too busy for the normal things in life.'

'What a shame,' murmured Annie, with all the genuine sympathy of one who came from a large family and was now intent on repeating her happy experience. 'Still, maybe you'll be able to make up for it now.'

Ros cringed at her friend's blatant prying, but Griff didn't seem to mind—she could hear a ripple of amusement in his voice as he answered, 'Maybe.'

'Are you actually retiring now?' Annie persisted.

'Not entirely. But I plan to take things a bit easier from here on.'

'Oh?' Annie studiously avoided Ros's eyes as she came back into the room. 'You know, I was just saying to Ros the other day, why on earth would anyone want to leave sunny California to come and live in wet old Yorkshire?'

An odd sort of smile curved his hard mouth. 'It isn't all sunshine,' he told her, an inflection of ironic humour in his voice.

'Well, no, I'm sure it isn't. You get those awful smogs, don't you? But even so...'

'I'm sorry, is my wife plaguing you?' enquired Paul, walking into the room just at that moment. 'She's the local directory, you know.' He dropped an affectionate kiss on her forehead.

'I am not!' protested Annie indignantly.

'Well, mind your own business, then,' he advised her bluntly, sitting down and pouring himself a cup of tea. 'Griff might not want to tell you why he decided to come to England.'

Griff shook his head. 'It's OK—there's no great secret about it. I just felt there was no longer enough scope for me creatively in LA. I've been increasingly involved with the scene in England over the past few years—sooner or later it was going to make sense to move over here lock, stock and barrel.'

'But didn't you mind leaving all your friends behind?' Annie persisted.

His eyes lit with teasing humour. 'Ah, there's this great new form of transport, you see. The aeroplane. Haven't you heard of them in Yorkshire?'

Annie giggled. 'Of course. But I still don't understand why you picked Arnby Bridge. I'd have thought London would have been more convenient.'

He shrugged lazily. 'London would still have had some of the fundamental problems of LA.' he explained. 'I plan to have a recording studio up here, and pull in the technicians I want for each separate project. That way I have total artistic control.'

'A *recording* studio?' gaped Annie. 'You mean we're going to have *more* stars tramping around our little village?'

He smiled. 'Not too many. I may even start to do a bit of work again myself—I've had talks about a film score that could be quite interesting.'

'There. Have you finished your cross-examination?' Paul enquired of his wife with teasing affection.

Annie gave him a sweet smile. 'Yes, thank you!'

'Good.' He grinned, and turned back to Griff. 'How's the work going up at the house?'

'Pretty well up to schedule. The weather's caused a bit of a hold-up, but there shouldn't be too many problems now. Which brings me to what I really came down for. I'm going back to the States tomorrow, but I'd sure like to return your hospitality this evening by inviting the three of you up to dinner.'

Paul shook his head regretfully. 'I'd really like to, but it's too short notice, I'm afraid. I'm on call this evening.'

'And I'm on the baby-sitting rota,' Annie put in. 'But there's no reason why Ros shouldn't go.'

Ros stared at her friend in horror. 'Oh, no, I . . . I couldn't, I . . .'

'Why not?' countered Annie, deliberately obtuse.

Griff was watching her, but it was impossible to read the expression in those dark eyes. Her bewildered mind sought desperately for some excuse, but she could find none. Surely they could all see that to go on her own was completely different from going in a threesome? Wasn't it? Or was she just being foolish again?

Before she could make any sense of it, Griff said evenly, 'Fine. I'll pick you up at about eight, then, shall I?'

She could only nod dumbly.

Paul put down his empty cup, and rose to his feet. 'Ah, well—tea-break's over. I'd better be getting off on my morning calls.' He bent and dropped a kiss on his wife's forehead, and ruffled his children's hair. ''Bye, you lot. See you later.'

Griff rose with him. 'I'd better be getting off, too. Thanks for the tea. I'll be seeing you. Goodbye, Ros,' he added, flickering her an enigmatic smile. 'I'll see you at eight.'

As soon as they were alone, Ros turned on her friend. 'Annie! That was a *rotten* thing to do,' she protested. 'I can't go out with him.'

'Why not?' countered Annie, bright-eyed with innocence.

'You know why not. That wasn't what he intended when he asked us. Now it'll look as if...'

'Well,' observed Annie, standing up and gathering up the teacups, 'he had plenty of opportunity to correct my mistake, but he didn't. I told you, he fancies you.'

'Annie, he does *not*,' insisted Ros heatedly.

Annie merely shrugged, a knowing smile on her lips as she walked into the kitchen.

As eight o'clock approached, Ros was becoming more and more agitated. 'Look,' she pleaded with Annie, 'tell him I couldn't come—tell him my Aunt Ermintrude is dying of appendicitis and I've rushed to her bedside.' Annie shook her head firmly, and Ros raised her eyes heavenwards. 'With friends like you, who needs enemies?' she sighed.

'Rubbish,' countered Annie brusquely. 'You're *dying* to go. I'm green with envy. Now, sit still, I'm going to put your hair up.'

By the time Annie had finished with her, Ros barely recognised her own reflection. She had coiled up her hair in an elegant style, and made-up her face, too— a fine sheen of foundation had faded out the freckles, and a touch of blue-grey shadow made her eyes look enormous. She would never be beautiful, and yet...

'There,' approved Annie, stepping back to admire her handiwork. 'Now, come on, hurry up and get dressed, he'll be here any minute.'

'Oh, Annie, I can't wear that,' she protested as her friend pulled a beautiful long black velvet skirt from her wardrobe. 'What if I spill something on it?'

'It'll dry-clean. And you can wear this with it—it'll suit you lovely.' She had produced a wrap-around style blouse of soft silk, black but splashed with darkly vibrant sapphire-blue flowers.

Ros sighed. There was going to be no getting out of this evening. And in truth she *was* looking forward to it—in that dry-mouthed, heart-pounding sort of way she used to feel as a child, standing in a fairground queue for the big dipper ride, her pocket-money in her hand.

The sound of the doorbell brought her head up sharply. 'He's here!'

Annie nodded as she heard the sound of his voice in the hall, talking to Paul. 'That's right.' She smiled reassuringly. 'You look sensational. Now go on down there and knock him dead!'

Griff was standing in the hall with Paul. He was wearing a well-cut dark suit, but to Ros he looked as sleek and dangerous as a panther. As she walked down the stairs he glanced up, and the arrested expression on his face as he saw her almost made her glance over her shoulder to see who he was looking at. A small thrill ran right through her, and she carried on down the stairs, a new-found confidence lending her an unconcious grace.

'Well! Good evening,' he murmured, letting his eyes drift down over her in undisguised apreciation.

'Hello,' she responded, hoping he wouldn't notice the slight tremor of nervousness in her voice.

Behind her, Annie supressed a giggle. 'Right. Off you go and enjoy yourselves. And don't worry about what time you get back, I'll leave the door on the latch.'

'Oh, I won't be late,' Ros assured her quickly. 'I'm afraid I might turn back into a pumpkin at twelve o'clock!'

'Oh, go on with you,' Annie grinned, pushing her forward. 'And you can stop gawping,' she added to her husband, taking his arm. 'You've seen Ros before.'

'Never looking as stunning as this!'

'It just goes to show what you can make out of a sow's ear,' laughed Ros nervously.

'You're doing it again,' murmured Griff as he helped her on with the coat Annie had lent her.

'Doing what?' she enquired, her smile a little too bright.

'Putting yourself down.'

'I like to get in first, before anyone else does it,' she told him lightly.

He laughed softly. 'Perhaps I shall have to teach you to see things differently.'

Ros felt her heart skid and begin to race out of control. But a small voice in the back of her head sharply whispered caution. In spite of his flattering words, she couldn't shake off the suspicion that he was playing some sort of game that was beyond her comprehension. He was rich and handsome—he had everything he could possibly want. Maybe he was bored. Maybe it amused him to pick on someone who was vulnerable, and break them into little pieces. She was going to have to be very careful.

The evening air was sharp with a frost that crisped the remaining pockets of snow. Griff opened the car door for her, and she slipped into the passenger seat, neatly avoiding brushing against him as he stood just a little too close. As he walked round to the other side and climbed in behind the wheel, she found that once again his nearness made her equilibrium falter.

It was essential not to look at his face. She found herself looking instead at his hands as he manoeuvred the powerful car away from the kerb. They were beautiful hands, pianist's hands, with long, tapering fingers, but they held a latent strength which showed as he lightly gripped and spun the wheel.

His skin was still golden from the California sun, and Ros wondered with a frisson of anticipation what she would do if he tried to touch her, maybe brush accidentally against her thigh as he changed gear. But he didn't, and she felt herself deflating with a contrary disappointment.

'Do you like Mexican food?'

'Mexican?' She blinked at him in astonishment. 'Well, I've never really tried it.'

'Well, it's time you did.'

'Why Mexican?' she asked, intrigued.

'Because my cook's Mexican.'

'Oh, I see. Well, that's logical, I suppose,' she mused, although his answer begged a dozen more questions.

He slanted her an amused smile, knowing that she was bursting with curiosity. 'Tino and Juanita have come over from California, now that I've sold my house out there.'

'Oh.' She nodded pensively.

A brand new set of gates had been hung across the entrance to the Priory, but Griff opened them at the touch of a button inside the car. Ros watched as they swung to behind them. 'Flash,' she murmured in a sardonic tone.

'Convenient,' he countered promptly.

Her mouth twisted into a humourless smile. 'You're really dragging us into the white-heat of the technological revolution, aren't you? Helicopters, recording studios, electronic gizmos to open gates!'

He lifted an enquiring eyebrow. 'You don't like progress?'

'Oh, is it progress?' she retorted, an edge of sarcasm in her voice.

He laughed with lazy mockery. 'Oh, I must have been mistaken, then,' he taunted. 'Do you know, I could have *sworn* I saw electric lights in your cottage—must have been some new sort of candle, I guess.'

For a moment she glared at him, but then an irresistible bubble of laughter rose to her lips. 'Oh, all right', she conceded. 'I'm just being a Luddite. I can't wait to see the house—I dare say you've got a laser display in the hall and satellite communication with the servants' quarters.'

'Not quite,' he promised.

The car drew to a halt, and he came round to open her door for her. Her nervousness returned as he took her hand to help her from the low seat, and she moved away from him quickly as soon as she was on her feet, with a murmured, 'Thank you.'

But if he was aware of her agitation he took no notice, merely standing aside to invite her to precede him to the front door. It opened as she stepped up to the porch, and she found herself being welcomed into that mediaeval English house by an ageing Mexican bandit wearing a bright yellow track-suit and running shoes.

Griff smiled at the bemused expression on her face. 'This is Tino,' he introduced her. 'Tino, say hello to Ros.'

The Mexican offered Ros his hand. 'Well, hi there, Ros,' he beamed. 'I sure am pleased to make your aquaintance.'

'H-hello,' she stammered, slightly overwhelmed.

'You want I should serve dinner right up, *patrón*?' he asked, turning to Griff.

'Yes, please.' He turned to help Ros slip off her coat, and handed it to Tino. 'Well, this is the hall,' he said, a lilt of teasing humour in his voice. 'As you can see, no laser lights.'

'No.' She gazed around in appreciation. The walls were panelled to the ceiling in oak, rich with the patina of centuries. 'Heavens, it must have cost you a *fortune* to have this restored—it was a real mess!'

'Oh, I've got a few dollars sloshing about,' he remarked with dry humour. 'I'm afraid some of the rooms aren't habitable yet,' he went on as he showed her into a room to the right of the hall. 'This will be the dining-room eventually—it's not too much of a trek from the kitchen—but for the time being it's doubling up as a sitting-room as well.'

It was a magnificent room. Wood-panelled like the hall, it was lit by half a dozen wall-sconces, and a real old-fashioned fire burned in a fireplace of baronial proportions. She slanted him a questioning glance. 'I thought you were having central heating put in.'

'Only in some of the rooms. Apparently it would damage the panelling if I had it in here.'

'Oh, dear,' she sympathised, her eyes dancing. 'How on earth will you manage?'

'Oh, I'll survive,' he drawled, grinning. 'Now, would you like a martini before dinner?'

'In England we usually serve sherry as an aperitif,' she advised him teasingly.

'Oh, do we? Well, I can't stand the stuff, so I'm afraid you'll have to make do without.'

'Oh, I'll survive,' she mimicked wickedly.

He shot her a laughing glance. 'That's fortunate,' he returned, sloshing a generous amount of gin into both glasses.

'I see you mix your martinis very dry,' she observed warily.

He raised an enquiring eyebrow. 'I'll put more vermouth in if you want it,' he offered with the air of one asked to commit sacrilege.

'No, that's all right, thank you,' she conceded. 'I don't like it too sweet.'

'Good.' He brought the glass to her. 'What shall we drink to?' he asked in that husky, velvety voice that made her heart flutter alarmingly. She retreated strategically to the other side of the fireplace.

'Oh . . . how about your new house?' she suggested, lifting her glass. 'Welcome to Arnby Bridge.'

'Thank you.' His smile told her that he sensed her nervousness, and was enjoying the power it gave him. He really was a most disconcerting man to be around. Those ebony eyes could laugh at one moment, and make her forget all her apprehension, but the next they would gleam sinfully, sending shivers of heat through her body.

To her relief there was a tap on the door, and Tino appeared, wheeling a dinner-trolley. 'Here we are,' he announced cheerfully. 'You like guacamole, Ros?'

'I don't know—I've never tasted it,' she admitted. 'Never?'

'I'm afraid the only Mexican food I've ever tried was chilli con carne, and that was out of a packet.'

Griff and Tino exchanged expressions of exaggerated shock. 'Juanita teach you,' Tino promised her reassuringly. He wheeled the trolley over to a small dining-table that had been set up in the oriel window overlooking the porch, and then with a cheerful, 'Eat well, Ros,' he withdrew, leaving them alone.

'Thank you,' she murmured, bemused. As the door closed behind him, she turned to Griff with a quizzical smile. 'He's quite an unusual butler,' she remarked.

'Yes. I'm afraid he doesn't quite look the part, does he?'

She gurgled with laughter. 'No, he doesn't. When did they arrive?'

'Yesterday.'

Ros nodded sagely. 'I thought they couldn't have been here long—I'd have heard all about them.'

He smiled. 'Ah, yes. The bush telegraph. I'm beginning to learn how that works. I went down to get some stamps this afternoon. By the way, I understand you're the best person to ask about the history of this house.'

The connection between the two statements wasn't lost on Ros. She might have guessed that the whole village would know that she was dining with Griff—dear Annie would never have been able to keep such a succulent morsel of gossip to herself.

'What do you want to know?' she asked as they took their places at the table.

'Everything, of course.'

'That's a tall order. It dates back to the twelfth century.'

'We've got plenty of time,' he pointed out with that beguiling smile.

She took a deep breath, trying to slow the disturbing flutter of her heart. 'OK. Well, the first part—the main hall—was built by the Knights Templars.'

'What, *the* Knights Templars?' he queried, suitably impressed.

'Of course. They were very powerful in those days—they owned huge estates all over Europe.'

He listened to her with a flattering degree of interest as they ate. She tried the guacamole with a certain amount of trepidation, but found that it was really quite delicious.

'Like it?'

She nodded. 'Mmm, yes! What sort of bread is this?'

'Not bread—tortillas. Here, have some soup—it's one of Juanita's specialities. Chicken and almonds, and other things she keeps secret.'

She slanted him a questioning glance across the table. 'They must think an awful lot of you, to come all this way to go on working for you,' she commented carefully.

He shrugged. 'Juanita's practically a second mother to me,' he told her in a voice that did not encourage further enquiry. But she didn't want to drop the subject, so she tried again from another angle.

'What do they think of Yorkshire?'

He smiled drily. 'That it's cold,' he supplied succinctly. 'You were telling me about the Knights Templars. What happened to them?'

Reluctantly she conceded defeat—it was evident that Griff was not going to allow her to pursue her enquiries any further. 'The Templars were suppressed in 1312,' she related. 'They were completely wiped out, and their lands given to other Orders. It was the Cistercians who turned this place into a Priory. They were the ones who built the other wing—you can tell the period from the shape of the windows.'

When they had finished their soup, Tino brought in the next course, a fluffy paella, yellow with saffron. 'You'll find this is a little spicier,' Griff warned her, reaching for a bottle of wine that had been standing in an ice-bucket on the corner of the table and filling her glass. 'You might like a drop of this to wash it down.'

'Thank you.' She took a cautious sip. It was a crisp *rosé*, with just enough character to complement the spicy food.

'Do you like it?'

'Yes. What is it?'

'You won't have heard of it. It's from my own vineyard in California. We don't make much of it, and even less gets sold—I usually end up giving most of it away.'

She toyed with her food, burning with curiosity to know more about his life in America, and why he had left it behind. But she was afraid that he would be angry if she asked him any more questions. She remembered him telling her once that he liked to guard his privacy, and even in the years when he had been a superstar there had been very little information available about his background.

'Carry on,' he prompted. 'You've only got as far as Henry the Eighth.'

She nodded. 'Right. Well, by 1540 most of the monasteries had been sold off to wealthy families, and turned into private houses. This house was bought by the Morvilles.'

'That was Earl Morville, was it?'

'No—the peerage came much later, in the reign of George the Fourth. But it was the same family.'

He encouraged her to keep talking as Tino brought in course after course, each one spicier than the last. She was grateful for the coolness of the wine, and didn't notice how much she was drinking—it wasn't until later that she realised it must have been too much. She only knew that she felt relaxed and comfortable, as if they were old friends who had always enjoyed this easy relationship. That warning voice inside her head seemed to have been lulled into a false sense of security.

'So didn't any of these Morvilles have the decency to stay and haunt the house?' Griff asked, his eyes smiling.

Ros gurgled with laughter. 'I'm afraid not. But they were a pretty wild bunch. Most of them drank themselves to death, or came to some other disreputable end. You wouldn't really want to share the house with a noisy, drunken ghost, would you?'

'I guess not,' he agreed, pretending to give the point solemn consideration. 'What happened after them?'

'The estate passed to some sort of cousins. Good, solid Victorians—you wouldn't want to be haunted by them, either. Dreadfully dull.' He nodded his head in agreement. 'I suppose there *might* have been some possibility from World War One,' she mused. 'It was a troop hospital then. And then after the war it was turned into a lunatic asylum for a while.'

'I hope none of *them* have lingered on!'

'Not that I ever heard of,' she reassured him, her eyes dancing. 'Anyway, it was closed in about the mid-thirties, and the house was empty for a bit, until the Second World War broke out. It was some sort of hush-hush place then. After that, the Salvation Army took it over and made it into a kid's home—it was still used for that when I was little. We often used to come up here to play. They closed it down about twelve years ago, and it was going to be made into a hotel, but the firm went bankrupt, and the bank's owned it ever since. They used to use it for meetings and things sometimes, but it's mostly been empty.'

'Quite a saga,' he remarked, topping up her wine-glass yet again. 'I never dreamt the place had been through so many changes.'

'Mmm. But it's happy now,' she told him, reaching out her hand to touch the cool stone of the window-sill. 'You can feel it—it's as if the house itself is alive.' Suddenly she realised how stupid she sounded, and blushed vividly. 'Oh, hark at me,' she laughed, picking up her wineglass and draining its contents in one nervous gulp. 'That was a lovely meal,' she added, smiling a little too brightly. Was she talking too much? The alcohol was swirling in her veins, making her feel deliciously light-headed.

'I'm glad you enjoyed it.'

Damn the man! Why was he smiling like that? Why did he have to look at her as if he were imagining what she looked like without any clothes on? And the awful thing was, she could feel herself responding, just as if his gaze were caressing her naked body. Could he tell? Was that why his dark eyes glowed, as if there were an elusive flame deep inside them?

CHAPTER FIVE

Ros blinked, startled, as the door opened again and Tino came into the room carrying a coffee-pot. How long had she been staring at Griff like that? At least if he found her behaviour odd, he made no comment. With an effort of will, she pulled herself together.

'You want coffee, Ros?' asked Tino, as friendly as if he had known her for years.

'Y-yes, please,' she managed to reply.

'Cream?'

'Yes, please—but no sugar.'

He grinned at her. 'You ain't on a diet, are you?'

She burst out laughing. 'Heavens, no! I'm far too skinny already!'

'Oh, I wouldn't say that,' murmured Griff, letting his gaze linger deliberately over the warm swell of her breasts, emphasised by the softly draped style of the silk blouse. She felt her cheeks tinge with pink under that dark-eyed survey, and he laughed softly. 'Do you know something?' he mused. 'You're the only woman I've ever known over the age of fifteen whom I can make blush so easily.'

She felt herself blushing harder, and tilted up her chin, angry with him for making her feel like a silly chit of a schoolgirl. Tino poured the coffee, and then collected up the debris of the meal and left them alone again. Absently Ros picked up a teaspoon to stir her coffee, gazing out of the window.

She could see the lights of the village twinkling further down the hill, but beyond it was pitch dark, except for the occasional twin beams of car head-lights on the road through the dale. The moon and stars were hidden by cloud, and the wild heather-banked moor was invisible.

'Have you finished stirring your coffee?'

Once again she was startled, realising that the spoon was clinking against the side of the cup. He was smiling, knowing exactly what it was that was dis-tracting her—he was causing it, quite deliberately. He was weaving spells in the air like a magician, binding her with invisible bonds until she would be com-pletely in his power.

She sipped her coffee, avoiding his eyes. It was rid-iculous—at her age, she really ought to know how to handle a situation like this with finesse. Thea would know exactly what to do—or even Chrissie, and she was only twenty-one!

She drew a deep breath to steady her nerves, and forced herself to speak. 'Well, now that you've had a chance to see the place properly, do you think you're going to like it here?' she enquired, hoping her voice sounded cool and sophisticated.

'I'm sure I shall.'

He was looking straight at her, as if meaning to imply that her presence was one of the main reasons why he was going to like it. Careful, Rosalind, she warned herself, not for the first time. This seductive charm was his stock-in-trade, and he seemed to be quite unscrupulous about the way he used it.

'I was afraid we might not have given you a very good first impression,' she burbled on. 'I mean last night. It was ... well, I suppose small-town bitchiness is the same the world over.'

He smiled. 'And so is jealousy.'

'Jealousy?' She fluttered her hands in a nervous gesture. 'Oh, I'm not really jealous of Thea,' she protested defensively.

'I didn't mean you were jealous of her—I meant that she's jealous of you. Jealous as hell.'

She shook her head quickly. 'Oh, no, I don't think so. Thea, jealous of me?' She could only laugh at the idea.

But Griff was nodding with certainty. 'I wouldn't mind betting that husband of hers was soon regretting that he'd chucked you over for her—and you can be pretty damn sure she knew it.'

Ros bit her lip, remembering all the times Stuart had tried to flirt with her after his marriage. She had hated him for it—and despised herself for giving him reason to believe she was that easy. But Griff's suggestion was ridiculous—she shook her head, dismissing the suggestion firmly.

'Oh, no. I'm sure you're wrong. I mean—Thea's lovely.'

He laughed softly. 'You know, for an intelligent woman, sometimes you can be remarkably dumb.' He was giving her that look that could melt a woman's bones. 'Surely you know it takes more than just a pretty face to really turn a man on?'

His voice was as soft and warm as velvet, and it was all she could do to resist his persuasive words. She flashed him a brittle smile. 'Of course—a decent figure helps, too.'

He shook his head. 'I'll tell you something about beautiful women. When you get right down to it, they're all pretty much the same. Within a couple of days, the impact of the way they look wears off, and then they're just boring. But you've got something different.'

'What's that? A million freckles and a brain?'

'A lethal combination!'

She really couldn't take any more of this—her hand was shaking so much, she had to put down her coffee-cup. 'Well, thank you for the dinner,' she managed with difficulty.

'You don't want to go yet.' It was a statement, not a question. 'You haven't seen the rest of the house. I want to know if it meets with your approval.'

'Oh...' She hesitated, knowing she should go, wanting to stay. 'Yes.'

'Good.' He smiled, and rose to his feet. 'Come on, then.'

For a moment she regretted her agreement. Her legs didn't feel strong enough to bear her weight. But when she stood up she found that, if she concentrated all her efforts on it, she could actually walk quite steadily.

The house was a warren of uneven corridors and odd flights of stairs. Ros could vividly recall games of hide-and-seek played here long ago with the children who used to call it home. Much of it still bore the scars of years of neglect, but careful workmanship was restoring it to its former glory.

They came by a roundabout route back to the main rooms on the ground floor. 'This is going to be the sitting-room when it's finished,' Griff told her, showing her into a room of magnificent proportions.

Heavy white canvas covered the floor, and two of the leaded windows had been removed and laid out for repair, while billowing plastic sheeting covered the gaps. Builders' tools were piled to one side of a hideous fireplace of yellowing scagliola.

'I don't remember that,' she remarked critically.

'No—there was another one in front of it—equally ugly,' he explained. 'But I'm assured that the original stone one is still there behind it—I hope it's going to be in as good condition as the one in the dining-room.'

She didn't want to risk standing still—that was to invite him to come too close—so she moved on to an archway from which the wide double doors must have been removed. 'What's in here?' she asked.

He followed her, switching on the light. It was another room of fine proportions, and the renovation work was somewhat more advanced than next door. The fireplace had already been stripped down to the original stonework, elaborately carved with heraldic designs above an elegant four-square arch. In the middle of the floor stood a large grand piano, covered with a dust-sheet.

'How on earth did you get that in here?' she asked curiously.

'With difficulty.'

She laughed, and moved on around the room. On each side of the fireplace the deep alcoves had been filled with bookshelves, and several crates of books stood waiting to have their contents added to those already in place. Casually she glanced along the shelves; she always liked to see what sort of books a person chose—she was sure it gave some insight into their character.

This was certainly an impressive collection—the more so because it bore the unmistakable signs of being well-used. It ranged from beautifully illustrated books of modern art to technical manuals of electronics. D.H. Lawrence rubbed shoulders with Wilbur Smith.

And then she came to a spine that jerked at her attention by its intimate familiarity. *By the Touchstone of the Law.* She drew it from its place, and turned it over. Her own image smiled up at her from the back cover—oh, what a long and painful session it had been to get one decent photograph!

Griff came up close behind her. 'You see, Rosalind Hammond—I recognised you before you recognised me. I'm one of your greatest fans.' He took a pen from his inside pocket, and put it into her hand. 'Will you autograph it for me?'

She stared up at him blankly—she was sure he was mocking her, though she could see no sign of it in his dark eyes. A faintly sardonic smile curved his mouth, and he lifted her numb hand to the page. She dashed off her signature automatically, and he took the book back from her, and put it carefully on the shelf.

'Thank you. I've got your others somewhere—they're probably still in the crate.'

She heard herself laughing almost hysterically as she gave him back his pen. 'I didn't think you'd be interested in history,' she remarked.

'Ah, that will teach you not to judge by appearances,' he chided her. 'Why shouldn't I be interested in history?'

'Oh, it doesn't fit the image somehow,' she teased audaciously. 'You know, the famous pop star!'

'Pop star!' he protested, laughing. 'One day, Miss Hammond, that tongue of yours is going to get you into very serious trouble!' He took her arm in a firm grip, and steered her over to the piano. 'Pop star, huh?'

He tossed aside the dust-cloth and, sitting down at the stool, ran his fingers lightly, lovingly, over the ivory keys. Then he began to play—a lively polonaise, holding her eyes challengingly as the rippling notes filled the room, filled her heart, making her want to dance.

Next he played a beautiful Brahms lullaby. The piano responded magically to his touch, as if it were a living thing, the melody swelling richly and fading to the softest whisper. She gazed in fascination at his hands as they caressed the music, a tingling fire running through her veins, and for one wild instant it was as though it was her body he was touching.

The lullaby ended, and he began idly picking out chords, weaving them slowly, and then with increasing certainty, into a melody she had never heard before. She watched him, feeling drawn to him in a way that was deeper and more mysterious than the physical longing that was becoming familiar in his presence.

'What's that you're playing?' she asked after a long moment.

'Oh, just doodling.' He played the refrain through again, this time in a minor key that gave it a haunting, elusive quality that caught at the heart-strings.

'It's lovely,' she whispered when he had finished. 'It's like the wind on the moors.'

He smiled at her. 'It needs a lot of work yet.'

'When did you learn to play the piano?' she asked curiously.

'At my mother's knee. I used to climb up on the piano stool almost from the moment I could toddle, and bash away at the keys. They couldn't keep me away from it. Eventually she decided she'd better teach me properly.'

'She must be very proud of you now,' she mused.

'She died when I was a kid,' he said, in a voice flattened of all emotion.

'Oh... I... I'm sorry,' she stammered, embarrassed.

He was quiet for a moment, his eyes unfocused. Then suddenly he crashed his hands on the chords. 'It's a long time ago,' he said almost flippantly, and began to play an up-tempo song that had been in the pop charts for weeks. It was as if a shutter had slammed down over that brief glimpse into the private world that he usually guarded so carefully.

He swung into another song, and she tapped her fingers on the piano in time to the music. He played several more modern songs, and then launched into the songs of an earlier era, sing-along songs, and she joined in, laughing with him. They belted out 'The Yellow Rose of Texas' and 'On Ilkley Moor Baht'at'.

Giggling, Ros plumped down on the piano stool beside him. 'Move up,' she demanded, wriggling into place, and with a theatrical flourish began playing her one and only piano piece, 'Chopsticks'. He joined in enthusiastically, and they played a rousing duet, finally collapsing in helpless laughter.

Almost before she knew what was happening, the laughter had turned to a kiss, and as he wrapped her up in his arms and drew her across his lap the kiss flamed rapidly out of control. She had no time even to think of resistance as he coaxed her lips apart and his plundering tongue invaded deep into the secret corners of her mouth.

With a deft hand he pulled the clips from her hair, raking his fingers through it so that it tumbled around her shoulders. Her head swam dizzily as she clung to him, returning the kiss with a hunger as urgent as his own. A hollow ache had awoken deep inside her, driving her on to her own destruction.

His hand slid slowly over her body, and her head tipped back as she gasped desperately for air. His hot mouth traced a scalding path down into the sensitive hollows of her throat, and she trembled with anticipation as she felt his caressing touch rise with unmistakable intent towards the aching swell of her breast. Those long, sensitive fingers cupped the ripe curve, and she moved against him instinctively, helpless in the grip of a primeval desire that was beyond all rational control.

He sensed her surrender, and she felt him loosen the wrap of her silk blouse and brush the fabric aside, and then he found the front clasp of her bra. She opened her eyes fleetingly as he unfastened it, dimly aware that she ought to be offering some objection, but she couldn't find the words.

She closed her eyes again, ashamed of her wantonness as she lay in his arms, the pink-tipped swell of her breasts naked beneath his eyes and hands. His mouth closed over hers, demanding all she had to give as with expert skill he fondled her, teasing the tender buds of her nipples until the pleasure pierced her brain like incandescent wires.

'I think we'd better go upstairs,' he murmured close to her mouth.

His words sank slowly into her brain, and abruptly she came to her senses, as if she had been doused with cold water. She struggled to sit up, turning her scarlet face away from him as she fumbled to straighten her clothes.

'What's the matter?' he demanded, his voice grating harshly.

Acid tears burned the backs of her eyes. 'I . . . I'm sorry,' she stammered.

'Sorry?' he hissed, his fingers curling around her wrist. 'You little bitch. What the hell kind of game do you think you're playing?'

'You're hurting my arm,' she protested in a small voice.

He let her go so violently, she almost fell off the piano stool. He stood up and crossed the room, leaning his hands against the wall high above the empty fireplace. 'You'd better go.'

Ros tried to stand, though her legs felt like water. She longed to feel his touch again, yet dreaded the consequences. 'Griff . . .' she whispered tremulously.

'I said go!' he snarled, turning to face her. The savage anger in his eyes made her catch her breath in fear. 'I've never forced a woman in my life, and I don't intend to start now!'

She fled from the room, and somehow found her way to the front door. The night air struck chill against her shoulders, and her footsteps were unsteady in Annie's high-heeled sandals, slipping on the frost-sheeted ground, but she ran from the house as if the demons of hell were on her tail.

She hadn't even reached the end of the drive when she heard the sound of the Jaguar's engine springing to life behind her. She was too out of breath to run any more so she walked, holding her head up, not even trying to fight back the tears that were running down her face.

The car pulled up beside her, and the door opened. 'Get in,' he ordered curtly.

'No, thank you,' she responded, with as much dignity as she could muster.

'Will you please get in?' he repeated in a strained voice. 'I promise not to touch you. I can't apologise with you marching along out there.'

His voice was rough, but there was an unmistakable note of sincerity in it. She hesitated for a moment, but she didn't have any will left to resist him. She got into the car. He didn't look at her; he kept his eyes on his hands as they gripped the wheel, the knuckles white.

'OK, I'm sorry,' he growled. He slid the car into gear and it moved slowly forwards, the gates swinging open to let them pass.

'S...so am I,' she responded in a small voice. 'I know that wasn't the sort of evening you'd intended. Annie and Paul should have been there.'

He cut her short with a derisive laugh. 'I only asked Annie and Paul because I didn't think you'd come on your own,' he told her. She stared at him in the darkness, and he slanted her a glance of sardonic amusement. 'What a mess of hang-ups you are, Rosalind Hammond,' he taunted softly. 'Maybe it's a good thing I'm going away tomorrow—I don't think I can cope with you.'

'I'm sorry.'

'And you don't have to keep apologising.' He drew the car to a halt outside Annie's, and reached over to take her hand. 'Look, I really am sorry about what happened just now,' he said, his voice deep with sincerity. 'I don't usually lose my temper when a woman says no.'

Her mouth curved into a wry smile. 'I don't suppose it happens very often,' she murmured shyly.

'No, it doesn't. And now I sound like a conceited bastard, don't I?'

She managed to meet his eyes, just for a second, and shook her head. 'No—I know it's true,' she whispered.

He smiled. 'There, that's better,' he said. 'Are we friends again?'

'Of course. If that's what you want.'

'It isn't *all* I want,' he warned in that smokily seductive voice. 'But I guess I'll have to settle for that— for now.' Slowly, almost thoughtfully, he lifted her hand, and gently laid a single kiss in the palm, and folded her fingers over it as if to hold it there. '*Adieu*, fair Rosalind,' he murmured softly.

She swallowed hard. 'Yes . . . er . . . goodnight,' she mumbled, searching frantically for the door-handle. He leaned across her and opened it, and she scrambled out.

'Don't forget your coat.' It was on the back seat, and he handed it to her.

'Thank you,' she mumbled. 'And thank you for the dinner—it was very nice.'

'I'm glad you enjoyed it.' His dark eyes glinted with satanic amusement, then he pulled the door shut, and she stood watching as if turned to stone as he reversed the car around in the wide part of the road. In a moment the red tail-lights had vanished up the hill.

The Osbourne household woke early. By seven o'clock the children were clamouring for breakfast, and the telephone was buzzing as Paul's patients rang for his attention. Ros had barely slept—all night she had tossed on the pillow, reliving every moment of her short aquaintance with Griff. As the first glimmer of dawn had crept through the curtains, she had slipped out of bed and gone over to the window, to gaze bleakly up at the pale grey sky, imagining his plane winging him far, far away from her.

She felt a little better after a warm shower, ready to face her friend's curiosity. The whole family was gathered in the kitchen, a bright, warm room at the back of the house. Little Peter was in his high-chair, his chubby little face covered in cereal as he gigglingly challenged his mother to get his teaspoon cleanly into his mouth. Annie paused from the game as Ros came into the room.

'Well, good morning, sleepy-head,' she greeted her cheerfully. 'What time did you get home last night?'

'Oh, not too late,' she answered with a bright smile, sitting down at the table and pouring herself a bowl of cornflakes. 'Hello, Lucy. What a nice T-shirt you've got on.'

'It's Thomas the Tank Engine,' the little girl told her, displaying the colourful design with pride.

'Well?' persisted Annie eagerly.

'We ate at his house,' Ros told her in a casual tone. 'He's got this incredible Mexican couple working for

him. They've just come over from California. Tino
and Juanita—I didn't meet Juanita, she was down in
the kitchen, but Tino...'

Annie clucked impatiently. 'When are you going to
see him again?'

Ros shrugged her slim shoulders with studied indifference. 'Oh, I dare say I'll bump into him when
he gets back from America.'

'Oh, don't be... Oh, Peter, stop spitting it out. It's
lovely—look, nice porridge. Come on, open wide for
Mummy.'

By the time Annie could turn her attention from
her small son again, Ros was engaged in a serious
conversation with little Lucy about the pleasures of
starting nursery school. Then Mrs Butterworth, the
daily 'treasure', arrived to add to the bustle, and Paul
had to hurry out to an early-morning call before
coming back to start his surgery. By that time, Ros
had finished her breakfast.

'Is that all you're having?' demanded Annie, regarding her empty cornflakes' bowl.

'Yes, thanks. That was plenty.'

'Oh, come on! No wonder you're so skinny! Sit
down and Mrs Butterworth will knock you up bacon
and eggs.'

'Yes, you sit down,' chimed in that good lady. 'It
won't take me half a jiffy.'

Ros laughed in protest. 'No, honestly, I've had
enough. I never eat much breakfast.'

'You never eat much, full stop,' scolded Annie, just
as if Ros were Lucy's age. 'I ought to make sure you
put a bit of weight on before Griff gets back—a man
likes something to get hold of, you know.'

'Well, I shan't be going out with him again, so it doesn't matter,' she responded firmly. 'Now, I'd better pop down home and see how things are. Where on earth am I going to find a plumber who'll be prepared to come right out here? They'll all be inundated with work at the moment.' She retreated to the hall to fetch her coat as she spoke, before Annie could question her further. She shrugged herself into her duffel coat and went back to the kitchen door. 'I'll see you later then. 'Bye.'

Annie's expression spoke a thousand things—curiosity, sympathy, the urgent desire to sit her friend down and give her some wordly-wise advice about men. But the children were fidgeting to get down from the table, so she had to contain her soul in patience, and content herself with, 'Mind how you go.'

The cottage felt cold and damp, a dismal place after the noisy cheerfulness of Annie's home. A quick inspection of the damage confirmed that it was going to need a major repair job. With a sigh she went back down to the hall and, setting the phone on her knee, she opened the directory and began dialling.

A dozen calls later, she had still had no luck. Everywhere it was the same story—'Sorry, lass, it's a bit out of our area.' One or two suggested she try again in six weeks—she was tempted to enquire if they were anticipating a massive landslide to move Arnby Bridge twenty miles or so to the east.

An unexpected knock on the door startled her. She put the phone down, and went to open it. A solid, grey-haired man in a well-worn but clean boiler-suit stood on the doorstep. 'Miss 'Ammond?' he enquired politely. She nodded. 'Understand you've had a burst, miss. I've come round to see what wants doing.'

'Oh!' Relief flooded through her as she opened the door wide to invite him inside. 'Which firm are you from?'

'Oh, we ain't local, miss. We're working on the old place up the hill.'

'The Priory?' she queried, puzzled.

'That's right. We've got a bit of a hold-up, see— waiting for deliveries—and the bloke that owns the place left a message to say as you'd got some urgent repairs, and to see what we could do.'

Ros hesitated. 'Well, yes, I have, but . . . if you're sure it won't inconvenience Mr Griffin at all?'

'Oh no, miss. He's gone abroad for a bit, so there's no rush. We'll be finished up there long before he gets back.'

'I see. And . . . he did make it plain that I'll be paying for the work myself?' she questioned nervously.

'He didn't say anything about that, miss, but if that's what you want to do, you'd best see the boss when he comes up. I'm just the foreman, see. Can I have a look upstairs, then?'

'Oh . . . yes, of course. Come in.' Still bemused, she followed him upstairs. That Griff should have taken the trouble to arrange this for her before he left! It was such a kind gesture, it almost made her want to cry.

Ros had never found it so difficult to concentrate on her work. At least while she stayed at Annie's she could make the excuse that there were too many distractions—if it wasn't the children, trotting in and out and wanting to 'help', it was Annie fetching her a cup of tea and staying to chat. Though if she was perfectly honest with herself, none of those things could have really taken her mind off her work if she had wanted to get on with it.

But even after she had returned home her progress was slow. To her relief, there was no difficulty about arranging to pay for the repairs to the cottage—she had felt she would have to refuse the offer if it had meant that Griff was paying. Fortunately the estimate was very reasonable, and the work only took a few days.

Usually she could finish the first draft of a manuscript in about three or four months, but as the weeks passed she was falling more and more behind schedule. She spent days walking over the windswept moors, wrapped up in her old duffel coat, enjoying the dismal melancholy of the weather and the landscape.

She chastised herself over and over for her foolishness. Jordan Griffin had women swooning over him wherever he went—one more would be just tedious. She had been no more than a game to him, to while away a few dull days. As soon as he had gone, he had forgotten all about her. If she had nurtured any crazy idea that he might write, maybe even ring her, disappointment set in like the wet spring as the weeks turned to months.

By the middle of June the weather had started to improve, and she had come to the conclusion that if she was going to find the inspiration she needed to finish her book, she was going to have to get away from Arnby Bridge for a while.

It seemed a shame to spend the loveliest season of the year confined in the grey streets of London, but

London was the only place she could do the research she needed. So she invited herself to stay with her old schoolfriend Shelley for a few weeks, and the warm summer days were spent within the hallowed portals of the British Museum reading-room.

It was cool and shaded in the vast, circular library. The small sounds of footfalls and pipe-scraping were absorbed by the banks of books that lined the walls right up to the glass dome of the roof. High up there the sun was shining, but down in the well of the room, among the catalogues and reading desks, the muffled quiet had a dreamlike quality that made it difficult to sustain any clarity of thought. She had doodled more than she had written this morning, and a mild headache was nagging behind her eyes.

Suddenly she became aware of an intrusion, a firmness of step, a briskness of movement. Heads turned, eyes stared disapprovingly. Ros glanced up—and felt the blood drain from her face. Strolling casually around the ring of catalogue shelves in the middle of the room, his whole presence jarringly at odds with the refined academic atmosphere, was Griff.

He was wearing a rather scruffy pair of jeans and a black and white sleeveless T-shirt emblazoned with the name of the Los Angeles Raiders football team. His skin was deeply tanned, defining the powerful muscles in his arms in a way that made her mouth dry. He was glancing down each radiating aisle of desks, his commanding height giving him an advantageous view.

What on earth was he doing here? And how had he got past the invincible security men in the lobby? Surely he didn't have a reader's ticket—who would have sponsored him? And yet it was almost unheard of for them to allow a member of the public in without one.

Instinctively she tried to shrink down behind her pile of books. But he had seen her, and was coming towards her, a purpose in his stride that confirmed that this was no coincidence. She had almost forgotten the way he walked, with those long, lazy strides, as coolly self-assured as a lion pacing out his territory.

He perched himself on the edge of her desk, and that famous smile curved his mouth. 'Hello, stranger,' he greeted her, in that familiar laconic drawl.

CHAPTER SIX

'HELLO,' she replied steadily, reaching for one of the largest books and pretending to study the index. 'What are you doing here?'

'Looking for you,' he countered with unnerving directness. 'Annie said I'd find you buried in here. How about lunch?'

Just like that? As if all he had to do was snap his fingers, and she would immediately drop everything else and do what he wanted? No—she was *not* going to let him walk back into her life like this and turn it upside-down again. 'I'm sorry,' she answered with admirable composure. 'I'm rather busy.'

'You've got to eat some time,' he pointed out reasonably.

'I've got sandwiches.'

He laughed softly, shaking his head. 'Am I still in disgrace for behaving so badly the last time we met? I had hoped I might have redeemed myself for that.'

She had to admit, when Jordan Griffin turned on the charm, it would be a hard heart indeed that could resist him. Reluctantly she returned his smile. 'All right,' she conceded. 'When I've finished what I'm doing...'

He nodded, satisfied. 'How long will you be?'

'About half an hour.'

'Fine.'

But he made no move to leave. After a few minutes, she was forced to say, 'Look, I can't concentrate with you sitting there watching me. If you want me to come, you'll have to wait outside.'

He grinned, and stood up. 'All right. But don't be long,' he warned, a teasing light in his eyes.

But there was no way she could go back to her work now. She sat for a while, staring blindly at the books in front of her, her mind a cauldron of emotions. Part of her was dizzy with happiness that he was back, and that he had actually come to find her. But another part was devoutly wishing that she could find a back door to slip out of, that she could run away and never have to see him again.

Damn the man, she thought viciously as she closed her books. Why *had* he come to find her? She had just been starting to get over the last episode, to convince herself that the attraction had all been on her part, that he had merely been responding out of kindness, to avoid hurting her feelings. But now...?

She walked briskly through the lofty marble halls of the museum, and out into the summer sunshine. He was sitting on the steps, leaning against one of the massive pillars. He stood up when he saw her, and gave her a smile of such genuine warmth that her heart lurched.

'That was quick,' he approved.

'Well, once you'd interrupted me I couldn't get my concentration back,' she grumbled, not quite trusting herself to relax with him.

He laughed—that low, rich laugh that she liked so much. 'Sorry,' he apologised cheerfully. 'Where do you fancy going for lunch?'

'There's quite a decent pub round the corner that does real ale and a ploughman's lunch,' she suggested.

He glanced at her in surprise. 'Is that all you want?' She nodded. 'OK, lead on. I don't know this part of town. I'm in your hands.'

It was a lovely sunny day—the sort of day to be strolling over the moors, not cooped up in the middle of the city. They managed to dodge through the heavy traffic on Southampton Row, and cut through the side roads to a small pub that Ros knew. It was decked with window-boxes and hanging baskets full of flowers, there were a couple of tables outside on the cobbled pavement, with bright sunshades, and they were early enough to find them still unoccupied.

'This is nice,' approved Griff, drawing out a chair for her. 'What will you have?'

'I'll have a half, please. But . . . are you sure you wouldn't rather sit inside?' she added diffidently. 'I mean . . . someone might recognise you out here.'

He smiled, shaking his head. 'Not many people recognise me now,' he told her. 'Especially this side of the Atlantic.'

'Oh? I'm not the only one, then?'

'Not by a long way,' he confirmed good-humouredly, and strolled into the pub to fetch their drinks. She sat back in her seat, closing her eyes and lifting her face to the warm sun. Whatever had kept Griff in America for so long, it seemed to have been resolved to his satisfaction. He seemed somehow more . . . relaxed. That hard edge of cynicism that had been so noticeable before had softened a little.

He came out with a tray bearing their glasses and two very substantial ploughman's lunches. 'Now, isn't this better than soggy sandwiches in that fusty old museum?' he asked her with a teasing smile.

'Oh, I suppose so,' she conceded, feigning reluctance. 'How did you get in there, anyway? Bribe the guards?'

'Of course not,' he protested, laughing. 'I simply engaged them in a rational discussion, and they agreed that my request was perfectly reasonable.'

'How long did that take you?' she enquired drily.

'Oh, not too long.'

Ros chuckled with laughter. So the irresistible Griffin charm could even work on the granite men who guarded the nation's literary treasure-house!

It was very pleasant sitting out there. Traffic was banned from this narrow street, and the cool, full-flavoured beer was very refreshing. The pub was getting busy, people were spilling out of the surrounding offices to take their lunch breaks, and Ros couldn't help noticing how many of the girls took a second glance at Griff. Not that they seemed to recognise him—it was just something about him that drew the eye.

'When did you get back from America?' she asked.

'At the weekend. Do you know, it was really nice to get back—I really felt as if I was coming home.'

She studied him covertly from beneath her lashes. Every line of his face had been etched into her memory, but memory had conjured only a shadow of that magnetic aura that surrounded him. It was like some elemental power, stronger than gravity itself. It took all her will-power to continue the conversation in the same friendly, neutral vein, and ask, 'Have they finished the work on your house yet?'

'Yes. I've had the stable-block converted into a re-cording studio, so I'll be able to work from home in future.'

'You're going to make records there?' she enquired with interest.

'Yes. That's why I've come down to London, to have a look at a couple of acts I might be interested in signing. What are you doing tonight?'

'Nothing, I...' He had caught her off balance. She had already decided that in the remote possibility that he should suggest taking her out, she would politely decline on the grounds of having too much to do. But she hadn't been ready for the question, and now she had trapped herself.

'Good. I'll pick you up at about eight, OK? Dinner first, and then we can go on to the club and have a look at these kids.'

'Oh, I'm really not sure...'

'Please. I'd like to have your opinion—someone outside the business, listening to them just as a casual listener to the radio might.'

'I don't really listen to the radio much,' she demurred.

'Even better. Come on, you can spare me one evening, can't you?' he coaxed.

Put like that, it seemed churlish to refuse—es-pecially after he had helped her out with the repairs to her cottage. 'All right,' she conceded. 'I'd better get back to work now, though,' she insisted. 'I've a lot to get through.'

'OK.' He stood up with her as she rose to her feet. 'Where are you staying?' She scribbled Shelley's address on a scrap of paper, and gave it to him. 'Eight o'clock, then. Don't be late.'

'I won't,' she promised. 'Goodbye.'

'But *who* are you going out with?' Shelley wanted to know. 'I didn't know you knew any men in London. Where did you meet him?'

Ros shrugged her shoulders with an assumption of indifference. 'He's just a chap that lives in Arnby. He's in London on business, and I happened to bump into him in the British Museum.'

'So what's his name, then?'

'Griff.'

Shelley's eyes widened, and Ros's heart sank. She might have guessed that Annie would have burned up the phone lines between Yorkshire and London with the news of the new arrival at the Priory. 'You don't mean Jordan Griffin?' she breathed. 'Oh, wow! Is he coming here to pick you up?'

Ros conceded a reluctant nod.

'Oh, wow!' Shelley fell backwards on to the bed in a spectacular faint. 'Oh, quick—he'll be here any minute. I've got to make myself look stunning!'

Ros smiled wryly as her friend scrambled off the bed and ran across the corridor to her own room. 'What's Graham going to think?' she enquired, referring to Shelley's husband.

'Oh, phooey to Graham!' declared Shelley blithely. 'It's not every day I get to meet the man of my dreams.'

Ros smiled wryly at her own reflection in the mirror. The man of her dreams—how true! If only he had remained there! It was a very dangerous flesh-and-blood man that she was dining with tonight. A shimmer of heat ran through her as she remembered the things that had happened the last time they had met.

She had done her best to make herself look presentable. She hadn't brought any suitable clothes to London with her, so that afternoon she had abandoned her dry old books—how on earth could she work, anyway?—and gone shopping down Oxford Street.

She had only intended to buy herself one dress, but she had found a fabulous boutique, and somehow... well, one thing had led to another. She had had to take a taxi home. Half the things were still on the bed—silk blouses, and a long velvet skirt, and piles of gloriously frivolous lace underwear.

She was wearing a very smart trouser-suit, black, with a fine gold lurex thread running through the fabric. Beneath she had on a simple little black silk vest-top, and Shelley had lent her a slender gold serpentine chain to wear around her throat. If only she could do something with her hair! Impatiently she tugged the brush through the thick curls.

The sound of the doorbell turned her to stone. 'That's him!' she heard Shelley cry excitedly as she raced down the stairs. She heard the front door open, and then voices in the hall—Shelley's excited, Griff's smooth and charming. If she didn't hurry, she told herself with a twist of self-mocking humour, she might find her friend had stolen him from under her nose.

He was looking cool and relaxed, in white trousers and a pale grey shirt, with a narrow pink tie, loosely knotted. He had rolled the cuffs back over his strong brown wrists, and as he smiled up at Ros she felt her heart flip over.

'Hi! You're looking good,' he complimented her casually.

'Thank you. I . . . I wasn't sure what to wear. Is this all right?'

'Sure. Come on, I've a cab waiting.' He flashed one of his devastating smiles at Shelley, leaving her squirming with delight as he led Ros out to the taxi.

Shelley lived in Stockwell, south of the river, and as Ros had expected they drove north, crossing Chelsea Bridge—her favourite of all the London bridges, with its elaborate cast-iron parapet and Victorian lamp-posts. 'Where are we going?' she asked curiously as they turned into the Kings Road.

'A place called Brannigan's—ever been there?'

She shook her head, her eyes wide—Brannigan's was famous as the place where all the celebrities gathered. Her stomach was fluttering with excitement. Something told her that this was going to be a night she would remember for the rest of her life.

The restaurant was in a side street just off the main road. It had a discreet frontage, just a window obscured by a rattan blind. Griff pushed the door open, and she stepped inside. Another couple had entered just in front of them, but their way had been barred by a neat, dapper little man who was insisting firmly that there was no room.

Ros glanced around the restaurant. It was a long, narrow room, with the tables crowded together so that it was difficult to move between them. The décor was elegant art nouveau, all ice-cream colours and smooth curves. In spite of what the little man was saying, the place was only half-full—but it seemed that one had to be famous, or beautiful, or both, to be favoured with a seat.

The couple in front of them conceded defeat, and as they turned to leave the little man turned to Griff, extending both hands in gushing welcome. 'Jordan! Greetings, greetings! You're looking great. When did you get back to England?'

'A few days ago. I'd like you to meet a friend of mine, Simon—this is Rosalind Hammond.'

Ros could almost see his mind flipping through its card index to identify the name. To her surprise, it registered, and she was favoured with a warm smile. 'Of course—I'm afraid I'm not much of a reader, Miss Hammond. May I call you Rosalind? But my mother loves your books—I think she must have read every one!'

'There's only been four,' she murmured, but he didn't seem to hear as he turned back to Griff.

'Where do you want to sit tonight, Jordan? I can find you a quiet corner if you'd prefer it.'

'Thanks, Simon, anywhere will do,' Griff responded genially.

He placed them at one of the most prominent tables in the room, obviously delighted to have Jordan Griffin enhance his restaurant's reputation as the 'in' place. All around them were faces as familiar to her from her television screen as her neighbours back home in Arnby, and they had barely sat down when the first of what became a constant stream of table-hoppers came over to join them for a few minutes.

It was like some teenage fantasy come to life. She sat smiling awkwardly as he introduced her to them, but she could tell by the look in their eyes that they were wondering what on earth he was doing with her—every other female in the place was either stunningly beautiful or incredibly famous.

She was grateful to be able to retreat behind a menu for a few moments while she gathered her thoughts. Although Griff seemed to be very much a part of this scene, she sensed a subtle difference in his manner with these people. And most of them were calling him Jordan; she could almost hear his own words, that first night she had met him—'My friends call me Griff.'

There was nothing to complain of in the food—it was evident that Simon Brannigan's reputation was based on more than just the glitter of his clientèle. They lingered over the meal for a long time, and by the time they were ready to move on they had collected a sizeable entourage of hangers-on.

The club that they were going to was in the West End, just off Wardour Street. In the overcrowded taxi Griff had dropped his arm around her shoulders, casually, just to make more space, but he kept his hold as they piled out on to the pavement.

The heavily built bouncer on the door recognised Griff on sight, and welcomed him with the enthusiasm of an over-large puppy. 'Go on in,' he invited generously. 'I wouldn't dream of charging you.'

The damp heat hit Ros in the face, making her fear that she wasn't going to be able to breathe. There were five young musicians crowded on to the small stage, attacking their instruments with such volume that it seemed to make every bone in her body vibrate, and the dazzling strobe-lights made her feel sick. She ducked gratefully into the shelter of Griff's arm as they skirted the crowded dance-floor to take over a table in an alcove close to the stage.

He slanted her an apologetic smile as they sat down. 'I'm sorry—this isn't really your scene, is it?'

She shook her head. 'Not really. It's a bit too noisy for me.'

'Never mind—we don't have to stay long. I can see what I need to see in twenty minutes.'

But, as the night wore on, it seemed he had forgotten his promise. One of the beautiful butterflies who had tagged on to their party had claimed his attention, and he seemed more interested in talking to her than in listening to the kids up on the stage. Ros's head was aching from the noise and those horrible lights, her eyes were stinging from the smoke in the air.

At last she just had to slip away for a few minutes to the ladies' room to get a breath of fresh air. She leaned back against the pink marble vanity-unit and breathed deeply, her eyes closed. Disappointment was gnawing at her heart. Although he had asked her out, his behaviour towards her had been no more than friendly. She had been right in the first place—he wasn't really attracted to her. He had just needed someone to come along tonight—probably as a shield against those predatory females they had met in the restaurant.

She heard the door open, and someone else came into the room, but she took no notice until a voice said, 'Excuse me, do you have a comb I could borrow?'

She opened her eyes, startled. 'Oh...yes, of course. Hang on a minute.' She searched quickly through her handbag and found her comb, and handed it to the girl with a smile.

'Thanks. Phew, isn't it hot in there? I just had to slip out for a couple of minutes.'

'Me, too,' agreed Ros, supressing a twinge of jealousy as she watched her comb her hair. Some girls just seemed to have all the luck. It wasn't only the perfection of her finely chiselled features and willowy figure. She had a sort of glow. Her skin was flawless, and if her artlessly tousled ash-blonde hair had achieved that natural look in a hairdresser's salon, she had at least got her money's worth.

It was hard to tell how old she was. At a first glance, Ros would have guessed about eighteen—but the low, rather husky pitch of her voice, and the worldly-wise expression in her brown eyes suggested that she could be at least five years older.

But though she would have put any of the glossy beauties with Griff's friends completely in the shade, she seemed to be much nicer than any of them. She had noticed that Ros was watching her, and smiled in a friendly way. 'What lovely hair you have,' she sighed enviously. 'Such a fabulous colour. I was thinking of having mine done red—blonde's a bit insipid really, isn't it? Do you think it would suit me?'

'Oh, but yours is lovely,' insisted Ros, surprised and flattered. 'I was just admiring it.'

'Were you really?' The girl sounded really pleased, as if in spite of the evidence in the mirror she didn't have much confidence in her looks. That was something Ros could sympathise with, and she felt drawn to the girl. 'Well, maybe I'll leave it alone for now. Have you been here before?' she added, handing back Ros's comb.

'No. And I don't think I'll be in a hurry to come again,' Ros remarked wryly.

The girl laughed—a low, musical laugh. 'I know what you mean. Who did you come here with, then?'

'Oh, just a friend.' A sudden, silly burst of pride made her add, 'Jordan Griffin. He's come to listen to the band—he's thinking of signing them.'

But if she had expected the girl to be impressed, she was quickly deflated. 'Oh, Griff,' she responded casually. 'I didn't see him come in. But it's so dark out there, you can't see a thing anyway.' Suddenly she seemed to remember something, and began to search in her handbag. 'I don't suppose you'd do me a favour, would you?' she asked diffidently. 'I expect he's forgotten all about it, but the last time I met him he promised to listen to a tape of my songs.' She produced a small cassette tape. 'Would you give it to him for me?'

'Of course,' agreed Ros readily. 'But why don't you come over and join us, and give it to him yourself?'

'Oh no, I wouldn't want to intrude. He's probably forgotten all about me,' the girl demurred modestly. 'But I'd really be ever so grateful.' She put the cassette into Ros's hand. 'My name's Stephanie Reeves— I call myself Stevie. I've put a little message on the end of the tape, so he'll know how to get in touch with me. Well, I'd better be going. Thanks ever so much—you're really kind.' She had vanished through the door before Ros could say anything else.

She turned the cassette over in her hand, frowning. She wasn't sure if Griff would be very pleased at having it given to him in this way. But she had seemed such a nice girl—and besides, he *had* promised to listen to the tape. She tucked it into her handbag, checked her appearance a last time, and went back to rejoin Griff.

'Where have you been?' he asked as she sat down beside him.

'Oh, I got talking to someone. She said she knew you—her name's Stephanie.'

'Never heard of her,' he remarked dismissively.

Ros looked up at him in surprise. 'She was very pretty—blonde hair...'

'I dare say,' he interrupted her, making it plain he wasn't interested. 'Are you ready to go?'

'Oh, yes!' she breathed in heartfelt relief.

It was so nice to get out into the fresh air—there must have been a shower of rain in the past hour, and there was a delicious coolness in the air. He dropped his arm around her shoulder again, and they strolled along in silence for a while. They walked down Dean Street and into Shaftesbury Avenue, deserted now, the litter of the day blowing in the kerb.

After a while he sighed deeply. 'Ah! I can't wait to get back to Yorkshire!'

Ros smiled up at him. 'What did you think of the band?' she asked. 'Are you going to sign them?'

He gave a cynical laugh. 'Oh, I expect so. They've got more hair than talent, but they're what the market's looking for at the moment.'

'If you don't like that sort of music, why do you produce it?'

'What makes you think I don't like it?' he enquired blandly.

'Do you?' she enquired, slanting him a dubious glance.

He hugged her closer. 'That's my Ros,' he teased. 'My breath of pure, fresh moorland air. I'm glad I brought you with me. Nights like tonight just remind me why I left Los Angeles.'

She could detect an edge of bitterness in his voice, and almost without forming the question in her mind blurted out, 'Why *did* you? Leave Los Angeles, I mean.'

She thought for a moment that he wasn't going to answer, and when he did speak it seemed almost as if he were talking to himself. 'I've lived there all my life. But it's a very empty town—nothing but palm-trees and smog. Everybody wants to be famous, and if they can't make it on their own they'll hang on to someone who's famous already, hoping to get a piece of the action. After a while, so many people have used you, you get to feel as if you're all used up.'

Ros felt her heart contract in sympathy, an emotion she could never have expected to feel for this cool, self-assured man. Instinctively she put her arm around his waist and hugged him. He caught her close against him, and as she lifted her face to look up at him en-quiringly he bent his head, and his mouth closed over hers.

Three months she had waited for this—three long, empty months. She responded to his kiss hungrily, surrendering blissfully to the fierceness of his demand, her body curved against his so intimately that she knew he must be able to read every quiver of desire in her.

She didn't even notice that he had hailed a taxi until it pulled up beside them at the kerb. He handed her into the back of it, and drew her into his arms again. Dark fires swirled in her brain, and she knew nothing but the swirl of his tongue deep into her mouth, the caress of his hand over the aching curve of her breast, until the taxi came to a stop. Only then did she realise that he hadn't taken her back to Shelley's.

The taxi had stopped outside a long, low block of discreetly luxurious flats—she had no idea where. It certainly wasn't Knightsbridge or anywhere like that— the road was lined with ornamental trees, and opposite there was a wide expanse of parkland.

'Where are we?' she asked blankly.

'Blackheath. I've a small apartment here—much better than using a hotel every time I come to London.'

Ros froze. Of course he had assumed that she was going to agree to spend the night with him—after the way she had succumbed to him in the taxi, it must have seemed to be a foregone conclusion. She hesitated as Griff held out his hand to her—but she was reluctant to argue about it in front of the taxi-driver, so she climbed out without demur.

But, as he took her arm to lead her up to the front door, she said quickly, 'Look, Griff, I'm sorry but . . . I'd rather go home—if you don't mind.' He looked down at her in surprise. 'I'm sorry, I should have said it before, but . . .' Her voice trailed away uncertainly.

He heaved a weary sigh, and stared up at the sky as if seeking patience among the stars. 'All right,' he conceded, his voice taut. 'My fault—I misjudged the situation, I guess. I'll call another taxi for you, OK? Will you let me offer you a coffee while you're waiting for it? I promise to behave myself,' he added quickly, holding up his hands in a gesture of innocence as he caught the wary look in her eyes. 'If you remember, I once told you I've never forced a woman in my life.'

'I don't suppose you need to,' she commented with a wry smile as she allowed him to usher her through the front door.

The flat was the most luxurious Ros had ever seen. It was like something from a glossy magazine—open-plan and split-level, with a thick white carpet and furniture upholstered in white leather. As Griff flicked a bank of switches beside the front door the lights came on, the curtains swished silently over the windows, and music poured from a stereo system.

'Wow!' she breathed.

Griff laughed. 'Have a seat,' he invited cordially. 'I'll call a cab for you, and put the coffee on, OK?'

'Thank you.' She hardly dared to touch the soft white hide of the big settee, but Griff dismissed her anxiety with a laugh.

'Make yourself at home,' he prompted. 'I assure you, it's all built to stand up to proper use—I wouldn't have anything that wasn't.' He leaned down over the back of her seat, just a little too close for comfort. 'Cream but no sugar, right?'

'Yes, thank you.' She eased carefully away from him, her heart thumping. Maybe she shouldn't have agreed to come inside, after all. She swallowed, trying to clear the tightness in her throat. 'Would you mind ringing that taxi now, please?' she insisted rather nervously.

His mouth twisted into a wry smile. 'OK, I'll keep my promise,' he conceded reluctantly. 'There's no need for you to be afraid of me, you know.'

She lowered her eyes, feeling that stupid blush stealing over her cheeks again. 'I know,' she agreed in a tense whisper. But she had every reason to be afraid—not of him, but of herself. She had been stupid to come to his flat—she had walked right into the devil's trap.

CHAPTER SEVEN

THE KITCHEN was a gleaming galley in one corner of the flat, half-open to the rest of the room. She heard him talking on the telephone, ordering her taxi, and heard him humming to himself as he made the coffee. By the time he came back to her, carrying two steaming mugs, she had managed to regather some semblance of composure.

He set the mugs on a low table, and lounged back on the settee opposite hers. 'The taxi will be here shortly,' he told her. 'So tell me, what have you been doing with yourself while I've been away? How's the book going?'

'Not too bad. I've had a bit of trouble with the first draft, but I've had a good couple of weeks' research down here, so I should be able to get on with it a bit better now.'

'What's it about? Or must I wait and read it?' he asked, accompanying his words with his most charming smile.

'Oh, it's to do with the time that Drake attacked the Spanish fleet in Cadiz, and delayed the sailing of the Armada by a whole year. It's about a Jesuit who becomes sickened by the intrigue of the Inquisition. He becomes a Protestant, and is persuaded to spy for the English. I was fascinated by what could motivate someone to turn traitor against his own country.'

'Why do you set all your stories in the sixteenth century?'

She smiled. 'When I was little, I thought we *were* living in the sixteenth century,' she told him. 'My Dad used to talk about people like Essex and Burghley as if they were still alive. Besides, if you write about the past, you can use real-life characters and events—it makes it much more interesting.'

'I'm looking forward to reading it,' he said. 'When will it be published?'

'Oh, it'll take at least another couple of months to finish it. Then the publisher might want some alterations—they usually do. After that ... Oh, it'll be another few months before it comes out.'

He nodded. 'When are you going back to Yorkshire?'

'I'm not sure—a couple of days.' Even though the coffee-table was between them, she still felt nervous. With a determined effort of will she made herself continue the conversation. 'What about you?' she asked him.

'Oh, some time this week.'

'Are you staying long this time?'

'I'm staying for good now.' He leaned back in his seat, and closed his eyes. 'I'm glad to be out of that nest of rattlesnakes,' he said, his voice suddenly weary. 'It's a devious kind of business, at times. My ex-partner, for instance, would sell his own mother to white slavers for a couple of bucks.'

'There are people like that in England, too,' she pointed out.

'Yeah, I guess so. But the whole thing's on a much smaller scale, everyone knows each other—you've an even chance of spotting a scam before you walk into it.'

'Why don't you just pack it in altogether?' she asked curiously. 'I mean, aren't there other things you'd prefer to be doing?'

'Such as?'

To her surprise, there seemed to be a glint of suspicion in his eyes. *Now* what had she said? 'Oh, I don't know,' she ran on, flustered. 'Why don't you try to make more time for your own music? Wouldn't you be happier doing that?'

'Possibly.' He was studying her face. 'What is it you want from me, Rosalind Hammond?'

She blinked at him in astonishment. 'Why should I want anything?'

His mouth twisted into a sardonic smile. 'Oh, everybody wants something,' he asserted with conviction.

'You can't mean that,' she protested horrified.

'Don't pretend to be naïve,' he sneered. 'I haven't quite worked you out yet, but I will.'

'I don't want anything from you,' she insisted, angry at his cynicism. 'What could I possibly want from you?'

'I suspect that you might want a great deal.'

She flushed scarlet. In a sense, that was true. She wanted the one thing he was most reluctant to give to anybody—she wanted his love. All these months she had been trying to tell herself that what she was suffering from was an adolescent infatuation with a pop star that would fade with familiarity.

But she couldn't deny the truth any longer. It was Griff she was in love with—not the famous image of

Jordan Griffin. But Griff was even more unattainable. And now he seemed to suspect that she was trying to trap him into something—did he think that was why she wouldn't let him make love to her?

With a click, the smoothly engineered machinery of the hi-fi came to the end of the tape that had been playing in the background. Griff uncoiled himself from his seat and stood up. 'I'll put another tape on. What would you like?' he asked her.

Suddenly Ros remembered the tape that the girl in the nightclub had given her. She reached into her bag and pulled it out. 'Would you play this?' she asked, handing it to him.

'What is it?' he asked suspiciously, turning it over and reading the hand-written label with a frown.

'That girl—you know, the one I told you about in the club,' she explained. 'She asked me to give it to you.'

'Oh, she did, did she?' Ros was puzzled by the glowering anger in his dark eyes. 'And you were happy to oblige. Can't I ever get away from it?' With an impatient gesture he tossed the tape across the room, where it clattered into a corner. 'Every talentless little nobody who wants to be a star, wheedling their way into my life, getting around my friends to introduce them...'

'She said...' began Ros nervously, vaguely feeling that she ought to defend Stevie, if only because hers had been the only friendly face in that hostile, arrogant crowd.

'Don't tell me,' he snapped, cutting her short. 'I can guess. She'd met me before, right? I'd said I'd listen to her demo, but she didn't want to intrude, so would you just give me the tape? Am I right?'

'I think you're being unfair,' she protested in a small voice, feeling all the more guilty because his assessment had been so accurate. 'She was a very nice girl.'

'Oh, I'm sure she was,' he sneered bitterly. 'That's how she conned you into giving me the tape.'

'You could at least listen to it,' she pursued. 'That wouldn't cost you anything.'

The temperature in the room seemed to have cooled by several degrees. 'All right,' he conceded, crossing the room and picking up the tape from the floor. 'I'll listen to it. And what will you do for me in return, eh?' He jabbed the tape into the hi-fi with a movement that was almost vicious, and the tinny sound of an amateur recording grated from the expensive sound-system.

'Well?' He was coming towards her slowly, menacingly. 'I'm listening to it. It sounds like a cat with its tail in a wringer, and it's probably ruining my speakers.' As she shrank back into her seat, he reached out his hand and grabbed her wrist, jerking her ruthlessly to her feet. 'And now one favour deserves another.'

He curled his fingers into her hair, forcing her head back. Her gasp of protest was smothered as his mouth descended cruelly on hers, crushing her lips apart. She tried to squirm away from him, but he was far too strong for her. His tongue swept into the defenceless valley of her mouth, plundering every secret corner in a savage invasion.

She tried to hold herself rigid in resistance, but her will was faltering, in spite of herself. She couldn't disguise her response. As her head swam dizzily, he swept her up into his arms, and strode over to the stairs.

'Griff, no!' she cried, trying to struggle. 'Put me down, please.'

He ignored her protests. He carried her straight up the stairs to the bedroom on the upper level. A huge double bed dominated the room, and he dropped her on to it. She tried to sit up, but he pushed her back. She stared up at him, tears starting to her eyes.

'You . . . you promised,' she protested in a choking voice. 'You said you'd never use force.'

'I just decided to change the habit of a lifetime,' he growled fiercely.

He caught her wrists as she tried to push him away, forcing her back on to the bed and crushing her beneath his weight. She bucked and twisted beneath him, but all he did was laugh in her face, as if he were thoroughly enjoying it. He was just waiting for her to exhaust herself.

'I'll scream,' she warned him, sobbing for breath.

'Scream all you want to,' he invited cordially. 'This is no jerry-built block where you can hear every sound from next door.'

'You mean it's sound-proofed?' she asked, aghast.

'As good as.'

She closed her eyes, and turned her face away from him, lying still. 'I didn't want it to happen like this,' she whispered, the tears spilling over and coursing down her cheeks.

To her surprise, as soon as she stopped struggling he let her go, rolling off her and flopping back on the bed beside her. 'Oh, lord,' he muttered, throwing his arm across his eyes, 'what the hell am I doing? I'm sorry, Ros. I didn't mean it. I just got mad.'

Cautiously she sat up, and stared down at him, still wary. He put up his hand and touched her cheek. 'I didn't hurt you, did I?'

'No. You just scared me a bit,' she admitted shakily. 'I thought you meant it.'

'I did, just for a minute.' He laughed, a trace of wry self-mockery in his voice. 'That's the second time you've almost driven me over the edge—I ought to steer clear of you.'

'I . . . I'm sorry,' she whispered tremulously. It seemed as if she were drowning in the dark, hypnotic depths of his eyes. Slowly his hand slid round her head to draw her down towards him. Their breath mingled, and their lips met again, melting together in a kiss that was all tenderness.

This time as his tongue swirled languorously into her mouth she yielded, and as his hand slid up beneath the thin silk of her top she didn't protest. His fingers curved possessively over the aching swell of her breast, and he lifted his head to smile down into her eyes.

'Mmm. You've got a fabulous body,' he murmured.

She blushed with pleasure. 'I . . . I always thought I was too skinny,' she confessed breathlessly. 'I'm practically flat-chested.'

He shook his head. 'Anything I can't hold in my hand is just waste,' he told her, easing aside the filmy lace of her bra-cup so that his expert fingers could tease the tender nipple into a taut bud of ecstasy.

Ros closed her eyes, and buried her face against his shoulder. She so much wanted to surrender, to stay here all night with him... But if she did that, the tenuous self-respect that she had rebuilt with such difficulty over the years would be shattered all over again.

As she wavered, unable to bring herself to a decision, the doorbell rang. 'My taxi!' She drew away from him, fumbling to pull her clothes straight.

'You're going?' he asked, surprised.

'Yes, I... Shelley will be wondering where I am if I don't go home.'

'Don't you think she'll guess?' he murmured, smiling.

She refused to meet his eyes. 'That's what I'm afraid of,' she confessed in a small voice.

He sighed, and as the bell rang again he stood up and helped her to her feet. 'All right,' he conceded. 'Maybe it's just as well.' He put his hands on each side of her face, and dropped a light kiss on the top of her head. '*Adieu*, fair Rosalind. Go on, you'd better hurry before he gives up and goes away.'

Shaken by that close encounter, Ros decided the next morning that, if Griff was going back to Arnby Bridge, she was going in the opposite direction. Since part of her book was set in mediaeval Spain, she had a ready-made excuse for herself—after all, she really *ought* to do the research at first hand.

It was the height of the tourist season, but she stayed well away from most of the tourist traps, rambling through sweltering Madrid, on down through Seville and finally to Cadiz, from where King Philip's

Armada had set sail four centuries ago on their ill-fated expedition.

It was there towards the end of August, that a letter from Annie finally caught up with her, announcing the healthy arrival of David Anthony Osbourne, seven pounds and two ounces. It was time to go home—why should she let Jordan Griffin keep her away from her friends?

She had forgotten that it was the Bank Holiday weekend. Heathrow was packed with crowds waiting for delayed holiday flights. She picked up her car from Shelley's, too eager to get home and get on with her work to accept her invitation to stay overnight, but as she sat impatiently in an endless line of crawling traffic on the motorway she wished she had stayed, after all.

The radio was tuned to a pop-music programme, and a bouncy disc jockey was compèring a panel discussion of the week's new releases. 'Right. Next one on the turntable—this is ''Obsession'' by Stevie Reeves.' Ros was so startled that she jerked at the wheel, causing the driver of the car in the next lane to give her a loud blast on his horn.

The music belted out, a raunchy, rocking sound, overlaid with a husky, sensuous female voice. It was unmistakable—that was the voice she had heard on the tape she had given Griff. She couldn't deny that it was really a very good song, and the panel enthusiastically agreed with her. The DJ announced that this was Stevie's first record, and that it had been written and produced by her new manager, Jordan Griffin.

So he had signed her, after all. Ros bit her lip. For the past two months she had refused to let herself remember that night in London, but now it all came flooding back. She could almost hear Griff's voice, soft and faintly regretful as he had said, 'Maybe it's just as well.' He had known that she was in love with him, and he had known what it would have done to her if she had stayed that night—and he hadn't wanted that on his conscience. Her heart ached so badly, it was difficult to hold back the tears.

And now he had met Stevie Reeves, and had changed his mind about her singing. That was hardly surprising! And if they were having an affair that wouldn't be surprising either. It was rather ironic, she reflected, that she had been the one who had brought them together. But she had always known that she couldn't have him for herself, and if it hadn't been Stevie it would have been someone else.

The sun was setting as she turned off the busy A1. The sky was a deep cobalt blue to the east, but to the west, above her beloved Dales, it was streaked with vermilion and gold. The road was quiet—most of the tourists tended to flock around Hardraw and Aysgarth, to the north, leaving some of the loveliest places to the locals, who weren't giving their secrets away.

She was just thinking how tranquil, how perfect it all was when the air was torn apart by the clatter of a helicopter. It buzzed over her like a giant gnat, and settled into the valley beyond the next line of hills. Jordan Griffin, 'commuting', she surmised wryly. How could she be expected to keep the man out of her mind, when he was continually intruding on her notice like this—his songs on the radio, his chopper shattering her peace, and no doubt his picture in the paper as frequently as ever?

It was almost dark by the time she reached Arnby Bridge. The lights of the village twinkled up the side of the hill, but her own cottage was in darkness. It seemed very empty, without even Cinders for company. She was tired after her journey, but really it was much too early to go to bed—and besides, she couldn't wait to see the new baby. She dumped her luggage in the hall, and drove straight on up the hill to Annie's.

'Ros! You look great! When did you get back?'

'About three minutes ago—I rushed straight up to see the baby as soon as I got home.'

'He's two weeks old,' Annie pointed out, laughing as she drew her into the hall.

'I only just got your letter. I've been on the move quite a bit.'

'Well, you're just in time—you can help me bath him.'

'Great. Oh, hello, you two!' she added, crouching down as Annie's two children came running out into the hall in their pyjamas. She swept her arms wide, hugging them both at once. To her surprise, little Lucy burst into tears. 'Hey, whatever's the matter?' she asked gently.

'You've come to take Cinders back,' the little girl sobbed.

Ros glanced up at Annie questioningly. Annie pulled a wry face. 'I was going to ask you ... would you miss her dreadfully?'

Ros smiled. 'It's my own fault for leaving her so long—I might have known this would happen. It's all right, Lucy,' she added reassuringly. 'She can stay here.'

She was rewarded with a melting smile. 'Oh, *thank* you, Auntie Ros! Come on, Peter, let's go and tell Cinders!'

The two children scuttled away, and their mother chuckled indulgently. 'You know, you ought to get married and have kids. You're really good with them.'

There was a trace of irony in Ros's laugh. 'Who'd put up with me?' she asked lightly. 'You know what I'm like when I'm into a book—I get completely carried away. We'd pass on the stairs, and he'd say, "Oh, I remember you—you're the one in the wedding photographs!" I don't really think that's a recipe for success, do you?'

Annie smiled, shaking her head. 'There's the right man out there for you somewhere,' she insisted. 'It's just a matter of finding him.'

'I'm perfectly happy as I am, thank you,' Ros declared firmly.

Annie clucked. 'I don't believe... No, Lucy, put Cinders down. Of course you can't take her to bed with you.'

'But she *wants* to come,' the child insisted, clutching the long-suffering cat to her chest.

'Mummy said no.'

'Hello, Paul. Congratulations,' smiled Ros, strolling into the sitting-room where the proud father was bouncing the newest arrival on his knee.

'Thanks.' He stood up and gave her a friendly kiss on the cheek. 'Well, here you are, little 'un. Your Auntie Ros has finally come to see you.'

He put the baby into her arms and she cuddled him close, loving his warm, milky smell and the perfection of his tiny fingers. Annie was so lucky! But fortunately the tussle of wills with her small daughter had distracted her friend's attention for long enough for her to bring her emotions under control.

'By the way, you've just got back in time,' Annie told her, her eyes dancing with excitement. 'Guess what's happening on Saturday? Griff's having a party!'

'Oh?'

'I can't wait!' Ros's damp response went unnoticed. 'There are all sorts of people going to be there—George Harrison, Eric Clapton, maybe even Diana Ross! It's to launch Stevie Reeves' new record. Oh, of course, you won't have met her. Griff signed her a couple of months ago. Her first record's just been released—Griff wrote it. It's really great! It's called "Obsession".'

Ros felt her jaw tighten, but she managed to keep her voice commendably level as she remarked casually, 'Oh, yes—I think I've heard it on the radio.'

'She's absolutely fabulous-looking—well, you'll see her on Saturday.'

'I haven't been invited,' Ros put in.

'Oh, don't be silly—you'll be going with us. Griff was asking only the other day when you'd be getting back. Did you see him in London, by the way? He said he might give you a call.'

'Oh, we had lunch. I think your son had better have his bath now,' she added, changing the subject. 'He's almost asleep.'

'Come on, then. You can carry him,' agreed Annie, always easily distractible.'

But she hadn't quite forgotten the subject, bringing it up again later when the children were all tucked up safely in their beds, and ruthlessly wringing a promise out of Ros that she would go to the party. Perhaps it was better not to protest too much—she didn't want Annie to remember that she had once harboured the illusion that there was a budding romance between herself and Griff. And besides, once she saw him with Stevie, it might be easier to come to terms with the reality of the situation, something she had been struggling to do ever since she had heard that record.

If she had been nervous about Annie's party back in March, that was nothing to the way she felt now. She was all of a dither, and barely able to eat a thing. She went shopping in York for a new dress, but she couldn't find one she liked, so she decided to wear the one she had worn to Annie's. That would convey some sort of message to Griff—that she wasn't so intent on impressing him that she minded about wearing the same dress. Not that he'd notice.

Paul and Annie came to pick her up at nine o'clock. Annie was positively bouncing with excitement. 'Oh, I can't *wait* to get there! The helicopters have been coming and going all afternoon.'

'I heard them,' put in Ros caustically.

'And you should have seen the cars we passed as we were driving down. Come on, are you ready? You won't need a coat.'

Annie burbled on happily as they drove up the hill, speculating on who was likely to be there. Ros felt the tension knotting in her stomach, but somehow she managed to make the right noises, and Annie was too carried away to notice that anything was wrong.

There were two heavyweight security guards on duty at the gate, and the drive was lined with several million pounds' worth of luxury cars. There were three helicopters parked on the lawn, and more security guards patrolling the grounds and at the front door.

There was a moment of awkwardness when it was found that Ros's name wasn't on the guest-list. 'Oh . . . no, it's all right,' she insisted quickly, feeling herself blushing under the professional suspicion of the guard. 'I'll go.'

'Rubbish!' protested Annie indignantly. 'What do you think she's going to do, for goodness' sake? Kidnap somebody?'

'I'm sorry, but it's more than my job's worth . . .'

'Is there a problem here? Why, hello, Ros—when did you get back?'

Her heart bounced alarmingly at the sound of that velvet voice. He was wearing a formal white dinner-jacket, but no tie, and the collar of his fine white shirt was unfastened, showing just a glimpse of the rough, dark hair that curled at the base of his throat. And the smile that he gave her took her breath away.

'Come on out back.' He invited them with a welcoming gesture to follow him through the house to the courtyard.

The scene that met Ros's eyes was like a set from a Hollywood movie—starring a galaxy of the most famous names in show business. The courtyard was framed on three sides by the rambling old house, which was now highlighted with brilliant spot-beams

from below to display the fascinating architecture to
the best effect.

The paved yard was dotted with dozens of tubs of
bright flowers, their perfumes mingling with Arpège
and Shalimar, and white-coated waiters—probably
security guards thinly disguised, to judge from the
muscular physiques most of them displayed—were
mingling among the guests bearing silver trays of
champagne and canapés.

'When did you get back from Spain?' Griff asked
her.

'Just . . . just a couple of days ago,' she managed to
respond.

'You didn't tell me you were planning to dash off
abroad,' he remarked, detaining her as Paul and Annie
moved off through the crowd. 'I tried ringing you,
but your friend told me you'd gone.'

Ros felt her heartbeat fluttering, and realised that
she was twisting her fingers nervously into the strap
of her bag. 'Oh, it . . . I'd been planning it for a while,'
she stammered, hoping that Shelley hadn't let it slip
that it had come as a surprise to her, too. 'I had to
do some more research.'

'How's the book coming on?' he asked in a friendly
tone.

'Not too bad.'

'Good. Well, come on over and get a drink.'

His fingers touched her elbow to draw her forward.
A shock of lightning ran up her arm, and she jerked
away from him instinctively. Their eyes clashed, his
puzzled and slightly angry, hers wide and startled as
a faun. She felt her cheeks flame scarlet—damn, why
did she *always* react like this around him? She choked

down the constriction in her throat, and started to apologise. 'I . . .'

'Ah, Griff, there you are. Harvey's looking for you.'

Stevie was like a vision. Her tousled ash-blonde hair and perfectly shaped scarlet lips were every man's sexual fantasy, her stunning figure was poured into a sheath of shimmering silver. She wrapped her beautifully manicured hands around Griff's arm, and smiled kindly at Ros.

'Hello. It's . . . Ros, isn't it?' she enquired with all that friendly charm that had first disarmed Ros. 'I'm so glad you've come. In a way, I have you to thank for all this.' She smiled up at Griff, and jealousy twisted like a knife in Ros's heart. Any lingering doubts she might have had died in the warmth of that smile. 'All of this' plainly included Griff, as well as the successful launch of her career.

'I . . . heard your record,' she forced herself to respond. 'It's very good.'

'Thank you. Griff wrote it for me. We're working on an album now. Working's the word!' What man could resist that throaty laugh? 'He's an absolute slave-driver.' The glow in her sapphire-blue eyes belied her words, and she brushed a speck of dust from his collar with one scarlet-tipped finger in a gesture that was oddly possessive. Ros felt the acid sting of tears behind her eyes, and turned away quickly to follow Paul and Annie.

It was hard to believe that she was really here, among all these famous, beautiful people. Trying to look as if she felt totally at ease. Tom and Thea were there, and Chrissie with her latest boyfriend, and the group of them drew instinctively together—like a wagon-train expecting an Apache raid, Ros thought with a twist of wry amusement.

Tom greeted her with a friendly grin. 'How was Spain?'

'Hot!'

'You didn't get much of a tan,' observed Thea smugly—her own slim body was an enviable shade of golden-brown.

'I would have done,' countered Ros, untroubled. 'If I'd stayed a few more weeks my freckles would have all run into each other.'

Thea returned her a thin smile, and promptly lost interest in her as Stevie swanned by on Griff's arm. 'Just look at that dress,' she remarked critically. 'How on earth did she get into it? It looks as if it's been painted on.'

'You can see *she* hasn't got any strap-marks on her tan,' added Chrissie in the same spirit.

'Mmm.' Tom expressed his approval enthusiastically, and Thea thumped him on the chest with her fist. 'She can have the last potato on my plate any day!'

'Well, if you fancy her so much, why don't you see if you can chat her up?' retaliated Thea loftily.

Tom shook his head. 'What, me compete with Jordan Griffin? You've got to be kidding—I don't back sure losers.'

Paul chuckled. 'You're well out of it, little brother,' he advised him. 'She'd eat you for breakfast and not even spit out the bones.'

'She's lovely, isn't she?' murmured Annie to Ros. 'She's very temperamental, though—Griff was telling Paul that they're falling terribly behind on the album.'

'Do you think he's in love with her?' Ros mused, hoping her voice didn't betray the misery she felt.

'I don't know. I think he must be, to put up with her the way he does.'

Ros couldn't keep her eyes from the beautiful couple as they circulated among the guests. Even in that glittering throng they seemed somehow extra special, like two beings from a higher planet who had come down to scatter their smiles like stardust over lesser mortals.

There was music playing softly in the background—Stevie's voice, singing Griff's songs. 'Obsession'. The words told of a girl destroying herself with an obsessive love for a man. Ros shivered, staring at the high bright stars, so remote in the summer sky, far above the ancient, ivy-clad walls of the old house.

Obsession. It was a dangerous word, and dangerously accurate. Impatiently she gave herself a little shake. It was stupid to be so melodramatic about it. She would survive—hadn't she always? But she had had enough of watching them together.

She couldn't leave yet, not till Paul and Annie were ready to go. They had gone off to dance, and Thea and Chrissie were united—for once—in disparaging every other female present. Cupping her champagne glass in both hands, she faded quietly back into the shadows.

CHAPTER EIGHT

THERE weren't many people in the house. Ros wandered aimlessly from room to room, remembering—moments from long-ago games with the children who had called this place home, but much more often moments from that one night in March when Griff had taken her on his guided tour.

So maybe it wasn't just chance that led her to the room where the grand piano stood. All the renovations were completed now. The walls were lined with books, and there was a fine Chinese carpet on the floor. The intricately carved stone fireplace was filled with bowls of yellow roses, and another bowl stood on the lid of the piano, mirrored in its glossy black surface.

She moved across the room, and lifted the lid over the ivory keys. The haunting theme he had played to her that night was running through her head, and she tipped her head on one side, trying to pick out the notes.

'I think you should stick to writing books—you'll never make a concert pianist.'

She spun round, her heart pounding. 'Oh, I . . . didn't hear you come in,' she gasped.

He smiled that dangerously attractive smile as he came across the room towards her. His fingers touched the keys, and the melody came to life, evoking a lonely, windswept night out on the wild moors.

She laughed wryly. 'You're right—I'll leave the piano-playing to you, and stick to writing.'

'Speaking of which, I have a complaint,' he chided, mock-severely. 'Two months you've been away, and not so much as a postcard.'

'I didn't know you wanted one,' she countered, trying to tease. 'Besides, you were in America for three months and never sent me one.'

'Touché.' His dark eyes drifted down over her body, and she felt her temperature rise as if he were caressing her. 'I like that dress,' he murmured. 'It suits you.'

'Oh, it's . . . practically the only one I've got,' she babbled foolishly. 'You've seen it before—at Annie's dinner party.'

'I remember.' He was coming towards her, but she couldn't back away. She couldn't move. 'So what did you get up to in Spain?' he enquired. 'You can't have been working all the time.'

'No, I had a bit of a holiday too,' she said brightly. 'Cadiz is where the Spanish go themselves—the beach was nice, just close to my hotel. Not that I can spend too long sunbathing—I burn too easily, and get all these horrid freckles.'

'They're not horrid,' he argued, his voice spinning a spell around her. 'I like them.' He brushed the tips of his fingers up her arm, electrifying her with shock. 'How many are there?' He began to count, touching each one lightly. 'One, two, three, four . . .'

Her breath was warm on her lips as she gazed up into those black-magic eyes. His hand closed over her shoulder, and his head bent towards hers. His mouth brushed hers, and the hot tip of his tongue flickered into the sensitive corner of her lips, making her senses reel.

His hand moved up to cup the ripe swell of her breast, his thumb teasing the hardening nub of her nipple through the silky fabric of her dress. She couldn't mistake the warning tension of male arousal in him, and her head swam dizzily. His arms folded around her, and his mouth plundered hers, demanding total submission. The fires inside her were raging out of control. She clung to him, responding helplessly to his skilful caresses.

'I'm glad you came back,' he rasped huskily. 'I was getting tired of waiting.'

He made a move towards the door, drawing her with him. But suddenly she realised his intention, and jerked away from him.

He frowned, his eyes glittering like black diamonds. 'No one's going to miss us for a couple of hours,' he rasped. 'So long as the champagne doesn't run out, they won't give a damn.'

She stared at him with misted eyes. 'No,' she managed to protest, her voice choking with tears. 'All you want is a quick...a quick...'

His smile held a promise of sizzling sensuality. 'Not a quick one,' he corrected her, his voice treacherously soft. 'I like it slow, warm and comfortable.'

'And you don't care who with, do you?' she snarled. 'Still, I suppose it doesn't matter with the lights out.'

'What?' His anger blazed. 'What the hell's the matter now?' he demanded, his steel fingers bruising her shoulders.

'Well, you hardly want to go to bed with me for my looks, do you?' she threw at him bitterly. 'You just think you won't have to put out too much effort—I'll be so overcome with gratitude I'll just melt in your arms.'

'You ...' He shook her fiercely. 'You and your damned hang-ups. Well, that's it—from now on, lady, I've had it with you.'

He slammed out of the room, leaving her trembling uncontrollably, silent tears streaming down her face. She squeezed her eyes shut, struggling to pull herself together. She had to stop herself crying—if anyone saw her like this ...

The door opened quietly, and she turned, startled, as Stevie slipped into the room. 'Oh, you poor thing,' she murmured in a rush of sympathy. She came over and put a comforting arm around Ros's shoulders. 'Have you got a hanky or something? Your make-up's all run, and your nose is red—you look awful!'

Ros caught her breath on a painful sob, clenching her jaw. Something about this girl was making her dislike her intensely, in spite of her gloss of charm. She fumbled in her bag for a tissue.

'I'm sorry,' Stevie went on. 'I can guess what happened.' Ros looked up at her questioningly. 'It's really my fault. But at least I know now that my tactics are working.' She smiled, just a little smugly. 'He's getting frustrated, you see. I won't sleep with him. I've no intention of being just another notch on his belt—I'm going to make him marry me.'

Ros stared at her in surprise.

'I didn't mind him going after you,' Stevie purred with total confidence. 'I'm expecting him to do that sort of thing a few more times before he admits defeat.'

Ros felt a chill of horror, as if she were staring at a beautiful but deadly poisonous snake. 'I . . . excuse me,' she mumbled. 'I'd better go and wash my face. My friends will be wondering where I am.'

She escaped from the room, unconscious memory guiding her to a small guest cloakroom under the stairs. Fifteen minutes later, her ravaged make-up repaired, she slipped back out into the courtyard—no one had even noticed she'd been gone.

It was a beautiful, golden autumn, but it was wasted on Ros. She had immersed herself totally in her book, resolutely putting every other thought from her mind. She would snatch a few hours' sleep—often not going to bed until it was light outside—and meals would consist of yogurts or bowls of cornflakes eaten in front of the green screen of her word-processor.

The weeks passed in a kind of blur, uncounted. She was refining and polishing the book, almost reluctant to let it go. When Annie rang her to ask her to stand as the new baby's godmother, she could hardly believe how late in the year it was.

'Ros, it's almost Christmas! The baby's more than three months old!'

'Already?' she asked blankly. 'But . . . I haven't seen him for weeks!'

'If I hadn't been so tied up, I'd have been down there to sort you out,' Annie pronounced in dire tones. 'Ros, you're impossible! Have you been eating properly?'

'Of course I have,' she protested, genuinely believing that she was telling the truth.

'I'm coming down there right now, and if I find that you've lost more weight, you're coming back up here until I've fattened you up,' Annie warned.

Ros cast a wry look around the cottage, seeing it properly for the first time in weeks. The curtains were still drawn, though it was three o'clock in the afternoon, and there was dust and discarded paper everywhere. 'No!' she gasped quickly. 'Not this afternoon, Annie. I'll come up to you—tomorrow, I promise.'

'Not good enough. I'll be there in ten minutes.' She put the phone down before Ros could protest further.

'Oh . . . damn!' muttered Ros. She was annoyed at the interruption, and yet . . . the book was really finished. She had been held in its coils for too long—suddenly she realised that it was time to break free, post off the manuscript, open the curtains, and breathe some fresh air.

She whizzed around the living-room at top speed, scooping up the litter into a big paper bag and piling her books neatly on the one side of the table. By the time Annie arrived she had the Hoover out and radio on, and her liberated spirit was singing.

'All right—before you say it, the place is a mess, I'm a mess, and yes, I have lost a bit of weight,' she announced cheerfully. 'What I need is a good wife.'

'What you need is a good husband,' scolded Annie, casting a critical eye around the room, not fooled by those last-minute efforts. 'Someone who won't let you neglect yourself like this.'

'I'm sorry. But it's finished—at least, I'm ready to send it off. I just hope the publisher likes it.'

'It is?' Annie hugged her. 'Oh, I'm so glad. Look, come on, leave all this and come home with me now. You can stay a couple of days—I'll tell you what, why don't we go into York tomorrow, just for a trot round the shops? Mrs Butterworth can look after the brats for me.'

'That's a good idea,' agreed Ros readily. 'Just give me a few minutes to parcel this up, and I can post it on the way to your house.'

'It feels like the end of term!' Ros spread her arms wide, and spun round, dancing like a child in the middle of the street.

Annie laughed at her. 'You're nuts!' she scolded.

'I know. Who cares? Oh, look—look at that!' In a shop window was a collection of fluffy toy dogs. 'They're the ones that sit up and bark when you clap your hands—look!' She dragged Annie into the shop, and insisted on demonstrating. 'I've got to get one for my new godson.'

'It'll scare the daylights out of him!' Annie protested.

'No it won't. I want one for myself, too. It'll be just right for me—it won't mind if I forget to feed it!'

Annie chuckled with laughter. 'Come on, hurry up, then. I've got to pick something to wear for the christening, and so have you. I'm not having you standing as my son's godmother in a pair of jeans.'

'Of course not,' agreed Ros cheerfully. 'I'm going to get something really posh. I'm a wealthy lady now, you know—I had a lovely big royalties' cheque a few days ago. I might even buy a hat! Who else have you got for godparents, by the way?'

'Tom and Griff.'

'Oh!' She smiled, though suddenly she felt as if she were sliding down a helter-skelter. She had started to make herself believe that the cut was healing, but one mention of his name could rip apart the careful stitches and open it up as deep as ever. 'Shouldn't you ask Stevie too, then?'

Annie's mouth thinned in dislike. 'No, thank you,' she returned tartly. 'Besides, she's not here—she's in America, touring.'

'Oh? She's doing quite well, then?' queried Ros lightly.

'Haven't you been listening to the radio or reading the papers? She's been at the top of the charts for three weeks with her second record, and her LP's doing well too. She's a star—and don't we all know it!'

'I didn't know,' mused Ros. 'I'm not surprised, really—she looked the sort who knows exactly how to get what she wants.' And that would include getting Griff to marry her, she reflected, remembering the girl's coolly calculating 'tactics'. How well were they working? Or had she been the one to succumb, and become just another notch on his belt?

The day of the christening was a beautiful, clear, crisp December day. A heavy overnight frost had gilded every twig with silver that sparkled in the pale winter sun, and the air was as fresh as chilled champagne. The village church was full of smiling faces—everyone in the village had come to the christening of Paul and Annie's baby.

The church had been built in the days when the profits from the wool-trade had made the area rich, and was much grander than the size of the present-day population suggested. Above the altar, a jewel-bright stained-glass window soared high into the vaulted stone roof.

Ros sat in the front pew, with Lucy snuggled up beside her. As she had promised Annie, she had bought something special to wear—a suit of soft mohair wool, in a beautiful sapphire blue, made by one of the top designers—and she had put up her hair beneath a chic little pillbox hat with a veil.

She had half turned in her seat to talk to one of the neighbours in the pew behind, but, though she was doing her best to pretend she hadn't noticed him, she was all too aware of Griff, seated not ten feet away from her along the pew. He was wearing a light oatmeal-coloured jacket that suited his dark colouring and emphasised the powerful breadth of his shoulders.

She hadn't seen him since the night of the party. Annie had innocently volunteered the information that he was working on the music for a film, and apparently he was as single-minded as she was herself when he was involved in something.

It was strange how, every time she saw him, she was startled afresh by the sheer physical impact of his presence. He was sitting back in the pew, laughing at something Paul had said, and as he turned his head he caught Ros's eye, and smiled.

She looked away quickly, and then immediately regretted that she had reacted like that—she should have simply returned him a friendly smile. But it was already too late to regain the moment. The organist had taken his place, and the rich music swelled, bringing the congregation to its feet. As it was so close to Christmas, the vicar had indulged them with a popular choice of carols, and the singing was lusty.

The christening came just before the end of the service. As Ros stepped out into the aisle to follow Annie and Paul to the font at the back of the church, she found herself walking between Tom and Griff. It wasn't too difficult to share a smile between the two of them, and she was able to present a semblance of far more composure than she felt.

The star of the proceedings, resplendent in the long white christening robe that had been passed down through Annie's family, screamed from the moment he was placed in the vicar's arms until he was handed back to his mother.

The service over, the guests drifted across the road to Annie's house, where a lavish buffet had been spread, crowned by a white christening cake. There was soon quite a crowd in Annie's spacious rooms, everyone chattering at once, and after the peace of her self-imposed isolation Ros was soon finding it all a bit too much.

She retreated to the hall, where she found Annie on her way upstairs with a rather grouchy small baby. 'What's up?' she asked. 'Anything I can do?'

Annie sighed. 'I'm just going to try to settle him down for a nap. He's been passed around and cooed over so much, he's worked himself into a thoroughly bad temper.'

'I'll take him,' offered Ros at once. 'I thoroughly sympathise with him.'

'Oh, would you? You're sure you don't mind?'

'I'd be grateful,' Ros asserted firmly. 'Come along, young man.' She took the baby carefully into her arms. 'Does he need feeding or changing or anything?'

'He might want a fresh nappy—they're in the airing-cupboard. And the nappy cream...'

'Don't worry, I know where everything is,' Ros reminded her. 'Go on, you go back to your party. We can manage, can't we, young man? Let's get you out of this silly frock, and then you can have a nice sleep.'

The nursery was two floors up, far enough away for the noise from downstairs to be muted. Ros murmured softly to the baby as she changed his nappy and dressed him in a comfortable sleeping-suit, and armed him with his dummy, then she settled herself in the rocking-chair to soothe him to sleep.

She was drifting in an idle reverie when she became aware that she was being watched. She looked up, startled, to see Griff standing in the doorway. He came quietly into the room, and sat down opposite her on a low stool.

'Hi,' he murmured, smiling that irresistible smile. He reached out his hand to play with the baby's tiny fingers. 'This is the first time I've seen you in months, and I find you with another man in your arms,' he joked gently.

She managed a smile. 'But you have to admit, he's rather a special man,' she pointed out, glancing down at the now sleeping child.

He nodded in agreement. 'I've never been asked to be a godparent before,' he told her. 'It was real nice of Annie and Paul—they're nice people.'

'Yes, they are.' She was watching him warily, but he didn't seem to be trying to flirt with her. He was just being . . . friendly. Well, maybe that answered her question—his relationship with Stevie must be going his way. 'Annie was telling me you're working on a film score,' she remarked conversationally.

'That's right—I took your advice about making more time for my own music. And you were right—I'm happier doing that. In fact, it's a good thing I've got Tino and Juanita to keep me in line, or I'd sit over it twenty-four hours a day.'

Ros laughed. 'I know—usually it's Annie who nags me to eat. And unless I get stuck, the housework piles up till the dust comes up to my knees!'

He laughed with her, and for the first time since she'd known him she felt herself beginning to relax a little in his company.

'Is that what you do when you get stuck?' he asked. 'Housework?'

'Sometimes. Or sometimes I walk. There are some lovely places around here—and not too many tourists at this time of year.'

He smiled. 'I'd like to see them—maybe you'll show me some time?'

'Of course,' she agreed readily.

'Good.' It seemed then that they had run out of conversation. Ros stood up, carried David over to his cot, and settled him down beneath his pale blue quilt. 'There,' she murmured. 'Goodnight, little one.' She smiled at Griff. 'We'd better leave him now.'

He nodded and followed her, tiptoeing from the room.

She closed the door behind them very quietly. 'Oh, well, I suppose I'd better go back into the throng, otherwise I'll be accused of being anti-social. The trouble is, I don't have much to say on the finer points of sheep-dipping or the price of ewes.'

Griff chuckled. 'At least it's a little better than how many million dollars some bozo's made on his latest album, or who's doing the best silicone cheekbones,' he countered drily.

Ros smiled up at him. 'You're probably right,' she agreed.

She had forgotten her casual promise to show Griff the local beauty spots, but the following morning she answered an unexpected knock on her door to find him standing there, his hands in the pockets of a black leather flying-jacket. He smiled down at her in a friendly way.

'Hi. I'm stuck again,' he announced. 'How about a nice brisk stroll to blow the cobwebs away?'

'Oh . . . yes, if you like,' she agreed breathlessly, her heart racing at the sight of him, even as her head reminded her sternly to be sensible.

'I'm not dragging you away from anything important?'

'No, of course not,' she assured him quickly. 'I was just trying to think of an excuse not to tidy out the cupboard under the stairs.'

'Then I'm happy to oblige.'

She smiled. 'Hang on, I'll get my coat.' She pulled on her old duffel coat—after all, it didn't really matter what she looked like, he wasn't going to be impressed anyway. 'Ready!'

It was nice to walk up over the moors with the wind in her hair. The pale sun gave little warmth, but the moors were still purple with heather, and overhead the kestrels soared high in the pale blue winter sky. They walked in silence for a while, Griff measuring his lazy stride to hers. The path followed the line of the beck that burbled down and under the bridge at Arnby. High on the moors it had carved a scar in the hard rock, plunging in a sheer drop to a dark pool below.

'This is my favourite place,' she confided. 'Not many people know about it.'

He nodded slowly as he gazed around. 'I can see why you keep it a secret,' he approved.

He sat down on a flat rock near the pool's edge, and she joined him, careful not to sit too close. It was taking a considerable effort to retain the note of casual friendliness, but she didn't want to spoil this precious interlude.

'How's the film score coming on?' she asked, trying to make conversation.

'Not too bad.'

'What's the film about?' she asked curiously.

'It's a kind of space odyssey—the special effects are stunning. So I'm using a lot of synthetic sounds, but on a symphonic structure.' She listened in fascination as he outlined the story of the film and his ideas for the music, humming her bits of the theme. She listened in total fascination—she didn't even notice the time flying past.

At last he rose to his feet. 'I've kept you out here in the cold long enough.' He smiled down at her, offering her his hand to help her up.

'Oh, that's all right,' she protested quickly, hoping he wouldn't notice how flustered she was by that fleeting touch. 'Has it helped?'

'It was just what I needed—fresh air, some nice scenery, and a bit of undemanding female companionship.'

She managed a smile, glad that he didn't know just how hard it had been for her to provide the latter.

'Maybe we could do the same thing again tomorrow?' he suggested as they strolled down the rocky path.

'Of course.' Her heart was jumping, but her voice was steady.

They parted where the path forked, he taking the short-cut that led over to the Priory. She watched him go, her mind in turmoil. He was offering her friendship, and that was something she would treasure. But it wasn't going to be easy—she was going to have to guard her heart every moment. Tomorrow...

It quickly became a routine, walking over the moors with him, just sharing the pleasure in the wild beauty of the Yorkshire landscape. As Christmas approached, she longed to ask him what his plans were for the holiday, but she didn't quite know how to raise the subject, afraid that he might think she was overstepping the invisible line that had been drawn in their relationship.

In the end she just blurted out, 'Well, it's Christmas in a couple of days. Is Stevie coming home?'

'No—why should she?'

She blinked at him in surprise. 'She's too busy to come home for Christmas?'

He shrugged his wide shoulders. 'It's no different from any other day of the week,' he responded, not a trace of emotion in his voice.

'But . . . *Christmas*,' she protested, shocked by his indifference.

'Oh, yes—the season of goodwill,' he sneered. 'So the fraction of the world that can afford it stuff themselves stupid while those in the poor nations starve. Everyone rushes round buying presents for people they can't stand, just because they expect to get something back.' He swung his hand in a dismissive gesture. 'The whole thing makes me sick.'

'Why are you always so cynical?' she asked sadly. 'Don't you believe anyone ever does anything except because they expect to get something back out of it?'

'I haven't met many people who don't,' he returned harshly. His hands were deep in the pockets of his flying-jacket as he gazed out over the bleak hills. 'Why am I cynical? I never found any good reason not to be.'

He went on, seeming to speak almost to himself. 'You know, when I was a kid, if anyone asked me what I wanted to be when I grew up, I used to tell them I wanted to be the biggest rock star in the world. I used to learn all the songs off the radio, and dream that I was standing up on a great big stage, in front of thousands of people, all screaming for me.

'And then one day it all came true. The noise hits you like a tidal wave. Playing a stadium, it's not like playing a theatre. It's not just the numbers—you can see them, all of them out there, and you just can't believe that they've all queued up and paid for their tickets, just to hear you play. You can feel they love you—people you've never even met. And all you want to do is give them something back.

'But then there are the others, the ones that don't want anything but to hang around you, and have you make them look good. They trade on your name, and smile in your face while they're ripping you off behind your back. Even Pa—he left town when I was about five or six, left Ma to manage on her own. Suddenly when I was making it big, there he was, back to find his long-lost son.'

He laughed bitterly. 'And then there were the women. In the music business, you can get hooked on booze and drugs, or you can get hooked on women. I chose the latter. In the beginning I was like a kid in a candy shop. But it doesn't take you long to realise that you're no more to them than some kind of trophy—the way the old white hunters used to stick tiger heads on their walls. Or maybe they liked to get their picture in the papers, or thought they could sing a bit themselves, and maybe you could help them. Yeah—I'm cynical.'

She stared at him, desolation in her eyes, unable to find anything to say. What was it he had said, that night in London? 'After a while, so many people have used you, you get to feel as if you're all used up.' What could she say? He didn't want sympathy, and how could she offer understanding? He had stood in the teeth of the gale all his life, while she had scuttled for cover at the first chill breeze, never daring to lift her head up ever since.

She followed him up the path, her heart aching. That brief glimpse into the dark side of his nature had only made her love him more—love the man, not the glossy, two-dimensional image she had adored for years. He was complex, fascinating—and so sexy that he took her breath away. But he could never be hers.

Maybe it would be better if she went away, after all. She could sell her cottage to Tom, never come back here... But she could never escape from Griff, no matter how far away she went—she might as well try to defy the force of gravity.

They walked for hours that morning, Griff seeming to forget to slacken his pace, so that it was all she could do to keep up with him. Hardly a word was exchanged between them until they got back to the fork in the path. Then he stopped, and smiled down at her crookedly.

'Thanks, lady,' he murmured.

'F... for what?'

'For lending me your moors.' He took her face in one hand, tilting it up. 'If it matters to you, Happy Christmas.' He bent his head, and brushed her lips lightly with his. Then he was gone, leaving her standing on the path as if she had been carved from the cold, hard rocks.

CHAPTER NINE

THERE was no sign of Griff at the Christmas-morning service in the village church, but Ros couldn't put his words out of her mind, even amid the warmth and laughter of Christmas dinner in the happy Osbourne household. She glanced around the room, resenting the shadow he had cast. Everything should have been perfect—what right did he have to spoil it with his cynicism?

'Penny for your thoughts.'

She glanced up with a smile as Tom came over and sat down beside her. 'I'm afraid I'd be cheating you,' she said. 'I wasn't really thinking anything—just enjoying myself.'

Tom slanted her a doubtful glance, but he didn't argue. 'What about that cottage of yours?' he asked instead. 'I'm still interested, you know.'

She hesitated. 'I don't know. It does need a lot doing to it.'

'I know that.' He sat forward eagerly. 'Come on—I'm encouraged. You've always turned me down flat before.'

She laughed, shaking her head. 'You're very persistent.'

'I'm hoping you'll get fed up with arguing with me, and sell.'

'You might not agree with the price I want. Or you might not be able to get a mortgage—building societies often aren't keen to lend on a property that old.'

'I don't need a mortgage—I've got the money Aunt Hattie left me,' he countered promptly. 'I can get the contracts drawn up in five minutes—all you've got to do is say the word.'

'Besides, I wouldn't want it to be just a weekend cottage. It ought to be lived in.'

'Of course. Most of my business is up here, with the farms and the villages. It'll make a good base. And when Thea and I are married...'

Ros stared at him, wide-eyed. 'Tom! You're *not* going to marry Thea?' she gasped.

He grinned. 'Yes, I am. Oh, I know she's got her faults—I ought to, we practically grew up together. But I know how to handle her.' He sounded absolutely confident, and on reflection Ros had to admit that he could be right. He would give Thea the stability she needed, while she could put some fizz into his life. They would make a good couple.

'The nub of it is, she doesn't want to leave Arnby Bridge,' he explained. 'I can understand that—after all, it's where all her friends are. But there's no way I'm moving into that house of hers. That was the first mistake John made with her—it was *her* house from the start, he was never allowed to even put anything down without being made to feel he was intruding.'

Ros nodded. Poor John—Thea's second husband. He hadn't been local—he was a successful businessman from Leeds, and he had never felt at home out here on the moors. But Thea had refused to move.

The marriage had been doomed from the start. Maybe it would be third time lucky for her—Ros found herself hoping that it would. There was a very nice side to Thea's nature, when there weren't any men around to be competed over. And she would certainly take care of Heather Cottage—she had a unique talent for home-making.

'Well...' she conceded thoughtfully. 'I'll think about it. If I ever *do* decide to sell, you'll be the first to know.'

She was quiet for the rest of the day, pondering on her conversation with Tom. Maybe it would be better if she sold the cottage and moved away—better than waiting around, clutching at every moment she could be close to Griff, like a scavenger lapping up the crumbs from Stevie's table.

She should go away, make a fresh life for herself. She was on the way to becoming quite an established author, she was making a lot of money—there had even been talk of one of her books being made into a television serial. She ought to move to London, where the action was. She could have a good time.

It was inevitable that Annie would notice her pensive mood. 'What's wrong?' she asked as they tucked the children up in bed. 'Haven't you enjoyed yourself today?'

'Oh, yes, of course I have,' Ros assured her quickly. 'I've had a lovely time—it was really nice of you to have me. I love watching the children unwrapping their presents.' She smiled wistfully at Lucy, snuggled down beneath her quilt, a brand new pink teddy-bear lying on her pillow next to the threadbare but still much-loved one she had had since she was born.

'Then what is it?'

Ros shrugged. 'I just sometimes wonder... if it's right. I mean, the way it's all so commercialised. When you think of how much people spend—surely it would be better to do something more worthwhile with all that money?'

Annie chuckled softly. 'You sound like Griff.'

Ros felt her cheeks flush faintly pink. 'Perhaps he's right.'

'What, that we shouldn't have turkey and Christmas pudding, or buy each other presents?' Annie bent to kiss her small daughter's rosy cheek. ''Night 'night, darling,' she murmured.

'I suppose it does seem... rather a Spartan attitude to take,' she mused. She laughed wryly. 'Anyway, I can't see Juanita and Tino letting him ignore it completely.'

'They've gone home to Mexico for Christmas, to see their family,' Annie told her, unaware that her friend might have any special interest in the subject.

'Will you read me a story, Auntie Ros?' A small hand reached for hers, a pair of blue eyes beguiled her.

'Of course. But then you've got to go to sleep—promise?'

The little girl nodded, and wriggled aside so that she could sit down on the edge of the bed. 'Please can I have Thomas the Tank Engine?' she asked, remembering her manners.

Annie smiled, and tiptoed from the room.

It was late when Ros left Annie's. 'Are you sure you won't stay the night, after all?' Annie asked as she shrugged herself into her coat—not the old duffel coat now, but a smart new one she had bought on her last trip to York—a real spy's trenchcoat, with a deep collar that she loved to turn up around her ears, pretending to be Mata Hari.

She laughed at Annie. 'Where would I sleep?' she enquired. 'You've got your parents here, not to mention Tom. I don't think I'd sleep very well on top of the wardrobe. Besides, you'll all be up at the crack of dawn tomorrow to go off to York.'

'All right. Have you got everything?'

'Yes. Thank you for all the presents, Annie. And thank you for having me today.' Impulsively she bent and kissed her friend on the cheek.

'Oh, don't be daft. You're always welcome here, you know that. Mind how you go, now—you haven't had too much to drink to be able to drive, have you?'

'Of course not!' Ros insisted with a pretence of indignation. 'Goodnight, Annie. Have a lovely time in York—let Paul's mum pamper you as much as she wants.'

'Oh, I shall, I shall!' promised Annie, coming to the door to wave her goodbye.

It was a beautiful evening. Beyond the village, the moors lay dark beneath the vast expanse of the sky. The stars looked such a long, long way away. She let herself into the cold cottage, and put her pile of Christmas presents down on the table in the livingroom.

She had put up a few decorations, and a small tinsel tree, but nothing could disguise the emptiness of the house—such a bleak contrast to the lovely day she had spent in the warmth of Annie's happy home. That was what Christmas was really all about—being with people you loved.

If Griff had ever had the privilege to see the light of wonder in a little girl's face as she woke on Christmas morning to find the stocking she had pinned to the end of her bed filled with presents, or watched the blue flames of burning brandy licking over a Christmas pudding, he could never be so cynical.

But he had never had that chance. She felt a little stab of sadness for the angry, lonely little boy who had dreamed of being famous, and had found out when the whole world loved him that he was lonelier than ever. She walked over to the cabinet where she kept her record collection, and drew out her favourite album. That classic aquiline profile, starkly lit against a black background . . .

She slid the record from its sleeve, and put it on the turntable. The sound of a bluesy harmonica filled the room, and then Griff's gravelly voice, so familiar. Her feet began to move to the driving rhythm as she sang along tunelessly to the words she knew so well— 'Heart like a rock . . .' A song about a man trying to pretend he was invulnerable, to hide a heart that was aching with loneliness.

On a sudden impulse, she reached into the box where she had put the left-over sheets of bright Christmas wrapping paper, and then ran upstairs to fetch the little fluffy walkie-talkie dog she had bought in York. She made it into a neat parcel, and then on a second impulse snatched up the small Christmas pudding Annie had pressed on her to eat on Boxing Day.

Quickly she checked her reflection in the mirror. Her dress was new, too—soft wool jersey in her favourite shade of blue, very demure, with a high rolled collar and long sleeves. She had liked it from the moment she had seen it—it was her favourite colour, and the subtle cling flattered her whippet-thin figure. Taking a deep breath, she went back out to the car.

Of course he was probably in bed—or busy in his studio, working on his film score. And of all the stupid things to take him for a present, that daft little toy— a man like Griff! She must be crazy. Half-way up the hill she almost stopped the car and turned round again, but then she decided to leave it in the hands of fate. If, when she got to the Priory, she couldn't see any lights, she would turn round then and drive home again.

There was a light in the last window to the left of the front door.

Ros drew the car to a halt in front of the porch, and took a deep breath. That room was the one with the books and the piano in it, and it was a long way from the front door. He might not hear her knock. If he didn't answer the door by the time she had counted to one hundred, she would get back in the car and go home.

She had got to eighty-nine when the door opened.

He clearly hadn't paid any attention to the fact that it was Christmas Day. He was wearing an old pair of jeans, and a pale-blue V-necked sweater, the sleeves pushed back over his strong brown wrists. A few dark hairs showed at the base of his throat, and the hardness of his thick shoulder-muscles seemed to be emphasised by the almost delicate softness of the lambswool. He stared at her in surprise. 'Ros! What on earth are you doing here at this time of night?'

She held out the present. 'Merry Christmas,' she uttered breathlessly.

He took it from her with a bemused expression. 'What is it?' he asked curiously. He held it up to his ear and shook it.

'Open it and see. It isn't much,' she added with a small shrug. 'It's stupid, really. I just . . . It was something I liked, and I thought you might like it too.'

His smile was warm enough for the cold, distant stars to feel the benefit. 'Come in,' he invited, holding the door wide for her.

'I brought Christmas dinner, too,' she added to cover her nervousness as she stepped inside. Why had she come? She *must* be crazy.

'Thank you.'

'I . . . I forgot the brandy butter.'

'Then we'd better see what we can find in the kitchen,' he responded cordially.

She followed him, her mouth dry and her legs trembling. He took her down a warren of corridors, until he pushed open a door and turned on a light, and she found herself in an enormous kitchen. It was in a kind of half-cellar, and the stone-vaulted ceiling was supported by thick pillars, giving it a crypt-like appearance—but there was nothing old-fashioned about the gleaming stainless-steel equipment. There was a huge double-ovened cooker, a tall freezer, and along the walls above the work-surfaces were ranks of pans and utensils of every kind.

'Welcome to Juanita's kingdom,' said Griff with a smile.

'Oh! I ... Will she mind me using it?'

'What the eye doesn't see...' he teased. 'So long as we're *very* careful to wash up and put everything back in its proper place. Now, what do you need? Butter, I suppose?'

'Yes. And sugar—icing sugar for preference. And an orange, if there is one. Oh, and brandy, of course.'

'Right.' He began looking in cupboards, like a mischievous small boy. Ros couldn't help giggling. 'There,' he announced when he had found everything. 'I'll go and fetch the brandy.'

Left alone in the kitchen, Ros refused to allow herself to have second thoughts about what she was doing. She took her coat off and calmly set about hunting for the utensils she needed. She popped the Christmas pudding into the microwave to warm up, and by the time Griff returned she had blended the butter and sugar, and was grating the rind of the orange into it.

He sat down on a stool opposite her, and rested his chin on his elbows. 'Mmm. Looks interesting,' he remarked. He dipped a finger into the bowl, avoiding her hand as she tried to smack it away, and stole a lick. 'Very nice,' he approved.

She had to concentrate hard to keep her hands steady as she measured out the brandy. By the time she had finished blending that in, the Christmas pudding was ready. Griff found a plate for it, and she turned it carefully out of its basin.

Griff breathed in the aroma. 'That smells delicious!'

'Annie made it,' she told him. 'She starts on them at Easter, and she always makes too many.'

'Well, it's lucky for us that she does,' he pointed out, picking up the plate. 'We'll eat this upstairs.'

She picked up the brandy and a couple of plates and spoons, and followed him up through the warren of steps and corridors to the room at the far end of the house—the music-room. Tonight a baronial fire blazed in the stone fireplace. She had been in this room twice before, and both times he had kissed her.

He slanted her a glance of quizzical enquiry, and she stepped forward nervously, holding out the brandy. 'Here—you have to set light to the Christmas pudding now, so that you can make a wish,' she explained.

'Ah! And shouldn't we have the lights off for that?' he enquired.

'Y... yes, I suppose so.' Her legs wouldn't support her any longer, and she sank down on the rug in front of the fire. He turned the lights off, so that only the flickering firelight illuminated the room, and fetching two brandy glasses came over to join her.

'So,' he murmured as he filled the glasses, and poured a generous slosh of the brandy over the pudding, 'what do I wish for?'

'Anything you like.'

'Anything?' His eyes were as black as sin in the soft glow of the fire. 'Then I wish...'

'No, you mustn't say it out loud,' she protested quickly. 'And you have to wait until the brandy's burning.'

'I see.'

With an air of solemn ceremony, he struck a match and touched it to the pool of brandy that had settled on the top of the pudding. It caught at once, and the ephemeral blue flames danced like fairy-lights. Ros gazed at them, letting them hypnotise her. She had been trying to pretend to herself that she didn't know why she had come—but she knew exactly what had brought her.

He seemed to know what she was thinking. As the flames died, he handed her a brandy glass, and lifted his in a toast. 'Merry Christmas,' he murmured smokily.

'Merry Christmas.' The rich, mellow spirit slid smoothly down her throat, spreading a glow of warmth into her bloodstream. 'You ... you haven't opened your present yet.'

He smiled regretfully as he reached over and picked it up. 'I haven't bought you anything.'

'It doesn't matter,' she answered softly. 'I didn't expect anything in return.' The significance of her words seemed to hang like a spell between them, binding them both motionless for a long moment. Ros was the first to move, busily attending to serving up the Christmas pudding.

Griff tore the paper off, and held up the fluffy toy in his hand. 'Well, well!' he drawled, his California accent suddenly stronger than ever. 'You're a cute little feller! Just the sort of pup I like—no puddles on my carpets!'

'He barks,' Ros explained. 'You just have to clap your hands.'

He put it down on the rug, and clapped his hands. The little dog sat up, and uttered his squeaking bark.

Griff burst out laughing, clapping his hands to stop the performance, and then clapping them again to start. 'Oh, that's great!' he enthused. 'I never saw anything like that.'

'I got him in York,' she told him. 'I'm glad you like him.'

'No one ever gave me a present like that.'

She swallowed another gulp of brandy, almost choking as the fiery spirit hit the back of her throat. 'Try the pudding,' she suggested in an unsteady voice.

They ate in silence for a while, Ros keeping her eyes lowered, aware of him watching her. It had been inevitable that it would come to this, sooner or later. Afterwards...but she'd think about that tomorrow.

'Where have you been today?' he asked. 'To Annie's?'

'Yes,' she nodded.

'That's a nice dress. Very demure. Blue suits you.'

She managed a smile. 'Thank you.'

He raised one eyebrow in amused enquiry. 'What, no protests? No reminder about your freckles?'

She felt herself blush. 'They've faded a bit now,' she murmured.

'What a pity. I rather liked them.'

She smiled shyly, remembering the way he had started to count them once. As if he was recalling the same moment, he put down his plate and reached across for her hand. She let him draw her towards him. 'You know, you really ought to be going,' he warned her, his voice suddenly huskier. 'If you stay much longer...'

Her heart was beating so fast, she felt dizzy. For an eternity there was no sound in the room but the crackling snap of the fire. And then, with a low groan, he drew her into his arms.

'I want you, Ros,' he breathed tensely. 'I can't believe the way you turn me on.'

His kisses burned across her trembling eyelids, and then found her mouth, parting her lips. Suddenly there was an urgency in him that demanded a response. She wrapped her arms around his neck, clinging to him as he laid her down on the hearthrug, surrendering beneath the plundering invasion of his kiss.

With deft fingers he began to unfasten the tiny buttons at the nape of her neck, and then she felt him draw down the long zip at the back of her dress. She yielded pliantly as he carefully stripped it off, her lashes lowered as he let his gaze drift slowly down over the length of her body, lingering possessively over the slender curves now hidden only by the filmy black lace of her underwear.

'Very nice,' he murmured huskily. She risked a glance up at him, and her heart almost stopped beating when she saw the dark fires blazing in his eyes.

His head bent over hers again, claiming her mouth in a kiss that melted her bones. His fingertips began to circle slowly, tantalisingly, over the smooth plain of her stomach, until he found the front clasp of her bra, nestling in the soft valley between her breasts. She caught her breath in trembling anticipation as he unfastened the hook, and brushed the delicate fabric aside.

A quiver ran through her as he began that lazy stroking again, tracing a spiral path over the aching swell of her small breasts. He was torturing her with pleasure, circling closer and closer to the tender pink peaks until she was reduced to a state of helpless abandon.

And then his mouth began to follow the same path, trailing scalding kisses over the delicate shell of her ear and down the vulnerable column of her throat. Her breath was hot on her lips as she moaned softly, her spine curling with sheer ecstasy as at last his lips found one taut pink nipple, swirling it languorously with his tongue and drawing it deep into his mouth to suckle it hungrily, pulsing white heat through her veins.

She ran her hands up under the soft wool of his sweater, thrilling at the power of the hard muscles in his back. The sheer overwhelming masculinity of his body was stirring an elemental excitement inside her, far beyond the reach of reason. She moved beneath him in wanton invitation as he slid his hands down the length of her spine, and in one smooth movement eased off her lace briefs, leaving her naked.

And then his long, sensitive fingers began to caress her with the most exquisite skill, stirring rippling notes of response from her fine-drawn nerve-fibres. Her ivory skin burned in the flickering flames of the fire as his kisses joined the refrain in sweet harmony, and she heard her own unearthly voice gasping, 'Please!'

He laughed, low in his throat, and his eyes smiled down into hers as his hand gently coaxed apart her slim thighs. She felt the caressing touch of his fingers, seeking the most intimate caresses, and a dart of pure pleasure shafted into her brain.

He took her tenderly, holding back the urgency that she sensed inside him. But as she moved beneath him in response he began to lose control, until she could only submit to the fierce demand, abandoning herself to the frenzied swirl of sensation that swept her up in a last magnificent crescendo that reverberated through her like the final notes of a symphony.

It had all been a dream—she couldn't really have done a thing like that. But then ... this wasn't her bed— she had plain white sheets, not this sophisticated dark grey. Very carefully she turned her head. She was alone in the wide bed, in the magnificent stone-walled room at the back of the house that Griff had chosen for his bedroom.

No, it couldn't have been a dream—it had been a night beyond all her dreams. After they had made love in front of the fire, he had picked her up and carried her up to bed, and made love to her again. Then he had brought her coffee, but it had gone cold as they made love again, finally falling into blissful sleep, entwined in each other's arms.

She lay back on the pillow and closed her eyes. She really ought to slip away now, discreetly. If Griff wanted her again, he would know where to find her. She didn't want to make him feel that she was making any demands on him. She had promised him that she wanted nothing in return—she had no right to ask for a change in the rules now.

With a small sigh she rolled out of bed. Her clothes were still downstairs in the music-room, and she looked around for something to put on. There was a navy blue Japanese-style cotton kimono over the back of a chair, so she put that on, tying the belt around her waist. It was far too big for her, and she giggled at the thought of what she must look like.

It took her a while to find her way around the warren of corridors and stairs, but as she reached the ground floor she could distinctly hear the rippling notes of a piano. It could only be coming from the music-room. She approached quietly in her bare feet, and stood by the half-open door.

Griff seemed to be totally absorbed in his music. Ros watched him, fascinated. The music was Mozart—the Elvira Madigan theme—and his fingers seemed to float over the keys. All trace of cynicism had been erased from his face, and a slight smile curved his mouth.

Suddenly he sensed her presence, and turned his head, not faltering by even a quaver. 'Hi,' he smiled. 'So you finally woke up?'

'Yes. I . . . I just came to fetch my clothes.'

'What's the hurry?' he enquired in a laconic drawl. 'You look great in that.' He held out his hand. 'Come here.'

Uncertainly she crossed the room, and let him draw her down on to his lap.

'And it has the added advantage,' he murmured, his eyes glinting teasingly, 'of not being too constricting.'

As his mouth claimed hers, his hand slid inside the neck of the kimono and his palm brushed over her breast. Already sensitively tuned to his touch, her body flooded with response, curving pliantly against him as he caressed her, surrendering without a murmur.

With a low groan he let her go. 'Breakfast first,' he decided, picking her up in his arms.

She gasped breathlessly. 'I can walk!'

'You haven't got anything on your feet, and the corridors are cold,' he pointed out. 'Come on—I'll give you a piggy-back to the kitchen.'

Laughing like an excited child, she climbed on to his broad back, and he carried her as if she weighed nothing at all, down the maze of corridors into the big kitchen, and sat her down on the big table.

'OK now, what have we got?' he enquired, investigating the fridge. 'Waffles! How do you go on toasted waffles for breakfast?'

'Sounds great!' she agreed. 'With oodles of butter.'

'No—maple syrup,' he insisted firmly. 'Now, where does Juanita keep the maple syrup?'

She sat watching him, wriggling her toes, as he pattered around the kitchen making breakfast. They ate in the kitchen, and afterwards they went back to bed again.

She never did get dressed, all that day or all the next. She kept thinking she really ought to go home, but it never seemed like quite the right moment—and besides, all the time he wanted her there, she wanted to stay. She knew that the dream would come to an end soon enough—and then she would have to try somehow to put the pieces of herself back together again. But at least she would have these few days to remember, for the rest of her life.

The second-best moments were when he played the piano for her. She loved to close her eyes and let the music drift over her—Strauss waltzes and Beethoven sonatas, John Lennon ballads and glitzy Ragtime.

And some of his own music, too. 'Remember this?' he asked her.

'Oh! That's the one you played to me when I came here before. Have you finished it?'

'No. I'll finish it now—it's for you. Let me see...' His brow furrowed with deep concentration, and then he began to murmur some words to the melody.

> 'When you're down and lonely, and the nights are dark and cold,
> You can be the richest man on earth, but what's the use of gold?
> Then you came out and found me, you didn't know my name,
> I touched your hand and watched you turn to flame.'

Ros blushed scarlet with pleasure. 'It ... it's beautiful,' she whispered.

'So are you—down deep, where it matters.' He reached for her hand. 'I'll finish it tomorrow.'

But, by the next morning, the song was forgotten.

CHAPTER TEN

THE NEXT morning Griff brought her breakfast in bed, with the morning papers. 'Here you are, sleepy-head,' he announced. 'Food for your tummy, and food for your brain. Let's see what the world's been getting up to behind our backs.'

With a yawn, she struggled up on the pillows. 'Give me that one,' she requested, holding out her hand for the tabloid. 'I'm not ready for too much intellectual stimulation just yet.'

She needn't have worried. Serious news hadn't been allowed to intrude on the festive spirit—the whole paper seemed to be given over to what the Royal Family and the casts of the popular soap-operas had been doing for Christmas and planned to do for the New Year.

But then she turned a page, and a small gasp escaped her lips. Smiling dazzlingly up at her was Stevie—hand in hand with a very handsome man. Next to the photograph was the headline, 'New Year Wedding for Star'. The story beneath it danced in front of her eyes.

Griff glanced at her enquiringly, and without a word she handed the paper to him. She couldn't look at him, but she felt him tense, and then he muttered a vicious curse under his breath, tossing the paper aside. 'I'm sorry, Ros. I have to go over to LA right away,' he said as he climbed out of bed. 'I've got to put a stop to this, and fast.'

She held her head up, and even managed some sort of smile. 'Of course.'

He hesitated in the doorway of the bathroom. 'Look, I'm sorry,' he said again. 'There isn't really time to talk right now...'

'That's all right—I understand,' she assured him, struggling at least to retain some dignity. She had known this would come, sooner or later.

A shadow of concern crossed his face. 'Will you be all right?' he asked gently.

She forced a light laugh. 'Of course I will. It's time I got home, anyway. I don't like leaving the cottage empty for too long in this cold weather—I don't want the pipes freezing up again.' There was a slight catch in her voice as memories flooded back. She scrambled out of bed, and began to get dressed. 'Besides, if anyone's been down there, they'll be wondering where I am. I don't want them sending t'search-party out over t'moors looking for me.'

He laughed at her playful assumption of a thick Yorkshire accent. 'OK. I'll see you when I get back.'

'Sure.'

He reached for her hand and drew her into his arms, holding her close against him for a long moment. She rested her cheek against the hard wall of his chest, forcing back the tears, refusing to let herself cling to him or beg him to stay.

'I'm glad you came,' he said softly. 'Mind how you drive home.'

She managed a brittle smile as she stepped back out of his arms. 'I've only got to go a mile,' she reminded him. 'You mind how you go—half-way round the world! I... I hope everything turns out all right,' she managed to add.

'Thanks.'

He was in a hurry to be going, so with a last smile she turned and left the room. She knew her way around the house now, and found the front door, though the tears she could no longer hold back were flooding her eyes, half blinding her. She made it to her car, but she never knew how she managed to drive home.

The cottage felt cold and empty, without even the cat to welcome her. She went straight up to her room and took off the blue wool dress, hanging it up carefully in the wardrobe. Then she crept between the cold sheets, and drew the covers up over her head like some small animal hibernating through the bleakest of winter.

She cried for two days, until her eyes felt as if they had been drenched in acid and her body ached with dull weariness. One thing she knew for certain—she couldn't be here when Griff and Stevie got back. She had no doubt at all that he would succeed in winning her back. Maybe he would even marry her—after all, if Tom was going to marry Thea, knowing what she could be like...

On the third day, she crept downstairs, wrapped in a blanket, and dialled Tom Osbourne's number. As he answered the phone she forced a smile into her voice. 'Hi. Never say I don't keep my promises,' she began in a rush.

'Ros? What is it?' he enquired, bemused.

'First refusal on my cottage—so long as you can get the contract drawn up today.'

'*What?* But . . . there are searches to do, papers . . .'

'Come off it, Tom. You've got the deeds in your safe—you did the transfer into my name when my father died. You know where the drains are and who has easement or whatever they call it.'

'Well, yes, of course, but . . . are you sure, Ros?' he asked seriously. 'I don't want you to rush into this and then start regretting it afterwards.'

'Oh, Tom, don't be so *solicitorish*!' she teased. 'I've been thinking about it for ages, and now I've made up my mind. And you know me, once I've made up my mind to something, there's no stopping me!'

There was a moment of silence, and then he said, 'All right. If you're absolutely certain this is what you want to do. I'll draw up the papers, and bring them over this afternoon.'

'Great!'

She hadn't planned to tell Annie until it was all settled, but ten minutes after her call to Tom the phone rang. 'Ros, what on earth's going on?' Annie demanded without preamble. 'Tom said you're going to sell him your cottage!'

'That's right.'

'But what's the rush? Where are you going?'

'London.'

'*What?* When did you decide that?'

'I've been thinking about it for a while, and I've finally decided to take the plunge,' she explained, the carefully rehearsed speech tripping off her tongue. 'Now I've made up my mind, I want to do it, before I chicken out and sink back into my comfortable old rut. It's my New Year's resolution!'

Her words had been well-chosen—they reflected what Annie had often said herself. 'Well... I suppose... You weren't going to leave without coming over to say goodbye, were you?'

She had been intending to do just that, but the wistful note in Annie's voice twisted her heart. 'Of course not,' she promised.

'Come to dinner?'

'All right. And I'm not going to another planet, you know. It only takes a couple of hours to drive up from London—I'll come and see you so often, you won't even realise I've gone away!'

She left Arnby Bridge the next day. She didn't have much to take with her—a suitcase full of clothes, a couple of boxes of odds and ends—books and papers, things like that—and her word-processor, loaded back into its original packaging. She had agreed a price for the contents of the cottage with Tom, and knew that she could trust him to settle the rest of the business honestly.

It was New Year's Eve, and it was raining steadily as she drove out of the Dales. She had no clear idea where she was going to go, and the windscreen wipers beat a dismal rhythm all the long miles down the motorway.

She didn't want to stay with Shelley. She wanted to be alone, an anonymous face in the crowded London streets. She found the perfect place—a bland guest-house in a bland street off Kensington Church Street, with a dozen faceless residents and a polite but uninterested staff.

No one seemed to notice that the guest in room eight was a robot—a perfectly functioning red-haired robot, who got up every day at a reasonable time, ate the food that was set in front of her, and wandered along staring blankly into shop windows until she was lost and had to get a taxi back.

She barely noticed the passage of time. Every morning she would flick through the newspapers without reading so much as her horoscope, and then cast them aside, an odd expression in her eyes. Whatever it was she was looking for, she hadn't found it.

There was a small lounge on the ground floor of the hotel, behind the dining-room, and it had a colour television. Every evening the robot would sit down in front of it, and watch right through to the epilogue. She seemed to be as interested in the international darts match as she was in the Hitchcock movie.

It was Friday evening—she must have been in London for about three weeks. The day had passed just like all the others, and now she was sitting in her usual armchair, staring dully at the television screen. It was one of those pop-music programmes, all laser lights and video technology.

Suddenly she froze as an all-too-familiar face appeared on the screen. Those arrogant features, those dark eyes... She stared at the screen, her heartbeat accelerating, her hands clenching tightly on the arms of her chair. The voice of the show's presenter was saying, 'Our next guest really needs no introduction. A comparatively recent exile to our shores, we've finally managed to persuade him to agree to an interview. Jordan—welcome.'

He smiled in acknowledgement. He was sitting, very relaxed, in a studio armchair—this was his world, and he was supremely confident in it.

'May I ask what is the position now regarding your former business partner, Bruce Nelson?'

Griff appeared to give his answer weighty consideration. 'I had suspected for some time that he had been resenting certain residual arrangements from the dissolution of our partnership,' he explained. 'The matter is now in the hands of my American lawyers. I deeply regret what has happened. Bruce was my friend for many years, and although we had some personal differences that led to us going our separate ways, I bore him no ill will.'

He was as good as a politician. If Ros hadn't known him so well, she would never have known he was lying, even though she could clearly remember the bitter things he had said about his ex-partner. Bruce Nelson... She frowned, trying to remember. That newspaper report—hadn't it said that Bruce Nelson was the name of the man Stevie had been going·to marry?

The presenter's next words confirmed it. 'Since Stevie Reeves called off her wedding plans and returned from America...'

Ros felt the acid sting of tears behind her eyes. So she *had* called off her engagement—it had been inevitable.

'. . . there has been considerable speculation.'

Griff lifted one eyebrow in cool enquiry.

'It's been rumoured that there may still be wedding bells in the offing,' the presenter finished with a nervous laugh.

Griff conceded a faint smile, and shook his head. 'Stevie and I have a very good working relationship, and I have a great deal of respect for her talent. But—to use a cliché that is frequently misinterpreted—we are just good friends.'

Of course he would lie about that—he had always fiercely guarded his privacy.

'Do you have plans to make a second album with Stevie?' was the next question.

'Yes. Now that she has finished her exhausting tour, she is taking a short break, but we hope to begin laying down the first tracks within the next few weeks.'

'And you'll be recording in your own studio in Yorkshire?'

'Of course.'

'And what of your future plans? You've bought a house here in England now—will you be settling permanently?'

He nodded. 'Yes, I will. I like England very much, I've been fortunate to make some very good friends here. This Christmas was, I think, the best I've ever spent.'

Ros sat up sharply. What was he saying?

The presenter was smiling, drawing the interview to a close. 'The song you're going to do for us now, is that from the new Stevie Reeves album?' he enquired.

'No. I'm not planning to record this one.' He smiled, stood up, and walked across the shadowed studio floor to sit down at a gleaming white grand piano, and looked straight into the camera. 'This one hasn't got a title,' he told ten million viewers. 'It didn't seem to need one.'

As the second camera drew in for a close-up of his long fingers rippling over the keys, Ros's heart almost stopped beating. He was playing the opening chords of the song he had said he had written for her. That smoky voice wove a spell into every word—the very words he had sung to her that evening in his music-room.

> 'When you're down and lonely, and the nights are dark and cold,
> You can be the richest man on earth, but what's the use of gold?
> Then you came out and found me, you didn't know my name,
> I touched your hand and watched you turn to flame.'

Soft strings swelled behind the refrain—just enough to fill out the melody.

> 'But since you went away the nights are cold again,
> I really need your tender love to take away the pain.

Lady, come on back to me, please don't stay away,
You know I just can't wait another day.'

She caught her breath on a silent sob. He seemed to be singing just for her.

'You didn't ask for anything, you gave it all for free,
No one else has ever done a thing like that for me.
Should have told you that I love you, it was just my stupid pride,
But now I need you back here by my side.'

The camera had zoomed in close on his face, and those dark, hypnotic eyes gazed straight into hers as he sang the chorus again.

''Cos since you went away the nights are cold again,
I really need your tender love to take away the pain.
Lady, come on back to me, please don't stay away.
You know I just can't wait another day.'

The tears were blinding her, rolling unheeded down her cheeks.

'Listen to me, lady, I played it much too cool,
I curse myself with every day for being such a fool.
I'm sorry that I hurt you, didn't mean to break your heart,

Now I know I loved you from the start.'

He really was singing just for her—he was calling to her, asking her to come back.

> ''Cos since you went away the nights are cold again,
> I really need your tender love to take away the pain.
> Lady, come on back to me, please don't stay away,
> You know I just can't wait another day.'

No one took any notice as she stood up and walked quietly from the room. The manager expressed only the faintest surprise when she told him she was leaving so late in the evening—but when she made no quibble about her bill he was all smiles and good wishes.

All the things that she had loaded into the car three weeks ago when she had left Yorkshire she loaded into it again, and set off for the long drive back up the motorway. She didn't bother to stop, not even for a cup of tea, and it was almost two o'clock in the morning as she drove into Arnby Bridge.

She hadn't even thought about what she was going to say to him. What if she was wrong? What if it had just been a pretty love song he had written for no one in particular? That was his job, writing those romantic words and making every woman in the world believe he had written them just for her. Maybe she was just making a complete fool of herself. If, when she got to the Priory, she couldn't see any lights, she would turn round and drive away again . . .

But as she turned in through the gate-posts she could see that a light glowed in the last window to the left of the front door. Her heart was in her mouth as she parked the car, and walked up to the front door. She could still turn round and run away...

She rapped sharply, snatching her hand away as if the knocker were red hot. Now she couldn't run away—her legs wouldn't carry her. She felt as if she were waiting to be executed. The light came on in the hall, and the door opened.

Nervousness switched on an over-bright smile. 'Hello,' she managed to say. 'I...'

Before she could say any more he had wrapped her up in his arms, and buried his face in her hair. 'I was afraid you wouldn't come,' he grated. 'I didn't know where to find you.'

'I... I saw you on television...' she stammered, overwhelmed by his response.

'I hoped you would.' He gazed down into her eyes. 'Why did you go off like that? I couldn't believe it when I got back and found you'd sold up and left.'

'I thought... when you saw the paper, and dashed straight off after Stevie like that... I thought you were going to try to stop her getting married,' she explained awkwardly.

He looked puzzled. 'Stop her getting married? Why would I want to do that? I don't give a damn who she marries—so long as she remembers she's under a professional contract to me. That was why I had to go—it said in that report in the paper...'

'That Bruce Nelson was her agent,' she finished quickly. 'Yes, yes, I understand that now, but...' She hesitated, finding the words difficult to say. 'I'd thought ... I'd thought it was because you were in love with her.'

He looked genuinely surprised, and then burst out laughing, hugging her close. 'You know, for an intelligent woman, sometimes you can be remarkably dumb,' he teased her.

She smiled up at him shyly. 'But...you *were* having an affair with her?'

'No, I was not,' he assured her firmly. 'Stevie was strictly business—and I never mix business with pleasure.'

He seemed to be telling the truth, but she was still afraid to let herself be convinced. 'She ... she's very beautiful,' she reminded him, a wistful note in her voice.

'So is a coral snake, but I wouldn't care to get into bed with one of those either. Whereas you, my love, are not beautiful at all,' he went on, swinging her up in the air. 'You're skinny, and covered in freckles, and positively riddled with hang-ups. I must have told myself a thousand times I didn't need the hassle. After that scene at Stevie's party, I promised myself I'd leave you well alone. But you'd got too much under my skin. You're one real special lady, you know that? You're smart, and sassy—and very, very sexy.'

He set her on her feet, holding her close in his arms so that she could feel the urgent pounding of his heart. 'If you hadn't come over here Christmas Day, I think I'd have had to come and get you,' he growled. 'I knew I'd been coming on too strong at the start, so I'd been trying to give you time, trying to get your confidence by acting like your best pal—but the temptation to throw you down in the heather... In fact, why are we standing here talking like this?' he added decisively, scooping her up in his arms. 'There's something much more important on my mind.'

She wrapped her arms around his neck as he carried her up the stairs. The incredible truth was at last becoming real to her. She had never thought she would be one of the lucky ones when it came to falling in love, but now she was the luckiest of all.

He set her down on his bed and she drew him down to her, tangling arms and legs as they rolled over each other, laughing at their own urgency that cursed the fumbling slowness of fingers with buttons, hungry for the heat of naked flesh against naked flesh.

The raw masculine power of his body took her breath away. She ran the palms of her hands up over the hard muscles in his shoulders, feeling herself to be deliciously soft and feminine by contrast. She could see herself reflected in his eyes, and love had made her beautiful.

In the three nights they had spent together, he had learned a lot about her—just the spot in the hollow of her shoulder where the brush of his lips could make her squirm with delight, the way she shuddered with pleasure when he swirled his hot tongue languorously around her taut pink nipples, and how to make her melt in helpless abandon with the gentlest of intimate caresses.

But she had learnt a trick or two of her own. She knew that there was a spot behind his ears that could produce a most interesting reaction when lightly kissed, and that if she danced the very tips of her fingers right down the length of his spine he almost exploded.

They romped on the bed like two wild animals, caught up in the mystery of spring, one minute laughing and teasing, the next searing with the flames of a passion so fierce it was almost frightening.

'I'm never going to let you go again,' he growled, trapping her beneath his weight. 'I'm going to keep you a prisoner here—lock you in the cellar and only let you out to make love to you.'

'You haven't got a cellar,' she objected reasonably.

'I'll have one specially built. Complete with spiders.' He tickled his hands all over her body, making her shriek.

'No, no—not spiders!' she pleaded, laughing helplessly. 'Anything but spiders.'

'Will you promise never to run away again?' he demanded, half-serious.

'I promise.' Suddenly it was all just too much, and the tears of happiness spilled over. 'Oh, I love you. I love you so much,' she whispered, clinging to him.

'Shush, my darling. Don't cry. I'll never make you cry again, I promise.' He kissed the tears away anxiously. 'I love you—as I never believed I could ever love anyone.'

To set the seal on his words, he took her with cherishing gentleness, and their mouths met in a deep and tender kiss to complete the union. The same elemental rhythm flowed through their veins, driving them on, into a land of swirling heat and soaring flames that fused their spirits for ever.

As they rested in the lingering afterglow, still tangled up in each other's arms, he smiled down at her lovingly. 'Every time I make love to you, it feels like the first time,' he murmured. 'And yet every time it gets better. Does that make sense?'

She gurgled with laughter. 'Does any of it make sense?' she asked him. 'What's going to happen if I get caught up in one of my books, or you're working on some music? We might not see each other for weeks at a time!'

He shook his head firmly. 'Oh, no. We're going to organise it better than that. Even if we both work all night and sleep all day, we're going to make time to spend with each other.'

'Right,' she agreed happily. 'Really it works out rather well—we've both got an obsession. If you were tied up with your music, and I didn't have my writing, I'd feel left out and at a loose end, and it would be the same the other way round. We're like port and blue Stilton—completely different, but absolutely great together.'

He laughed uproariously at her simile. 'Port and blue Stilton?' he repeated. 'That's the first time I've ever been likened to a lump of cheese!'

'No, I'm the cheese,' she pointed out. 'Look, I've got the blue veins.' She showed him the delicate tracery beneath the pale skin inside of her wrist. 'And you're the port,' she added, nestling down comfortably in the crook of his arm. 'Strong, and dark . . . and guaranteed to get me flat on my back every time!'

He chuckled richly. 'Mmm—an interesting thought,' he mused. 'I wonder what our children will be like?'

She stared up at him, startled. 'Children?'

'Of course. You want children, don't you?'

'Oh, yes!' she breathed. 'Oh, of course I do!'

'Good. I'd like five. Not just yet, though—I want you to myself for a little while first. We'll get married as soon as we can fix it—where would you like to go for our honeymoon? I think Japan would be nice— the shores of Lake Fuji.'

She was still staring at him, hardly daring to believe what she was hearing. 'You want to marry me?' she whispered in astonishment. 'I ... I only thought you meant ...'

He caught her up in a loving hug, almost squeezing the breath out of her body. 'You thought I'd be satisfied to live in sin with you?' he teased, laying her back on the bed and beginning to caress her again. 'You know, for an intelligent woman, sometimes you can be remarkably dumb!'

Somehow the media found out about the wedding, though Griff did everything he could to keep it secret. It might have been someone from the local Registrar's office, but Ros was inclined to suspect it was Stevie. She didn't know how the girl had first taken the news—she hadn't been there when Griff had told her. By the time she had met her again, any anger or jealousy was hidden behind that flawless mask. Her revenge had been to try to make sure that the quiet wedding they had planned would be ruined by an invasion of Press and television. But Griff had neatly side-stepped the problem.

Ros peeped nervously into the tiny side-chapel in the south transept of the church. It was just the right size for the twenty or so guests who had been invited. The flickering glow of hundreds of candles danced on the mellow stone walls, lending the atmosphere a very special warmth and intimacy. The rest of the church was in darkness, every whisper echoing mysteriously in the lofty stone vaults of the ceiling. It was just a few minutes after midnight, and all the reporters were sleeping unsuspectingly in their beds.

'Do I look all right?' she whispered tensely to Annie.

Her friend smiled reassuringly. 'You look lovely,' she promised, brushing down a fold of the exquisite ivory satin dress and adjusting one of the tiny silk flowers that held the heavy lace veil in place. 'Go on.'

Paul, immaculate in a grey morning-suit, offered her his arm. 'Annie's right,' he told her quietly. 'You've positively blossomed these past few weeks.'

Ros smiled up at him happily. She no longer felt awkward about such compliments. She saw herself through different eyes now—Griff's eyes. As she stepped into the chapel he turned from his place beside the altar, and she felt her heart soar as he smiled at her. In the past few weeks he had stilled all her doubts and anxieties. She understood now that none of the pretty faces that surrounded him in the music business meant a thing to him. He loved her.

The ugly duckling moved like a swan, proud and graceful as she walked down the aisle. Griff reached out and took her hand in his, and the beautiful candle-lit service began.

VOWS   *LaVyrle Spencer*   **£2.99**

When high-spirited Emily meets her father's new business rival, Tom, sparks fly, and create a blend of pride and passion in this compelling and memorable novel.

LOTUS MOON   *Janice Kaiser*   **£2.99**

This novel vividly captures the futility of the Vietnam War and the legacy it left. Haunting memories of the beautiful Lotus Moon fuel Buck Michael's dangerous obsession, which only Amanda Parr can help overcome.

SECOND TIME LUCKY   *Eleanor Woods*   **£2.75**

Danielle has been married twice. Now, as a young, beautiful widow, can she back-track to the first husband whose life she left in ruins with her eternal quest for entertainment and the high life?

These three new titles will be out in bookshops from September 1989.

W●RLDWIDE

Available from Boots, Martins, John Menzies, W.H. Smith, Woolworths and other paperback stockists.

ROMANCE

Next month's romances from Mills & Boon

Each month, you can choose from a world of variety in romance with Mills & Boon. These are the new titles to look out for next month.

THE POWER AND THE PASSION Emma Darcy
GOODBYE FOREVER Sandra Field
BRIDE FOR A PRICE Stephanie Howard
DARK MOON RISING Dana James
THAT CERTAIN YEARNING Claudia Jameson
FREE SPIRIT Penny Jordan
A SPECIAL ARRANGEMENT Madeleine Ker
WITH NO RESERVATIONS Leigh Michaels
FROZEN ENCHANTMENT Jessica Steele
LEAP IN THE DARK Kate Walker
HIJACKED HEART Sally Cook
TRUST ME, MY LOVE Sally Heywood
LOVE'S PERJURY Marina Francis
BITTER SECRET Carol Gregor

Buy them from your usual paperback stockist, or write to: Mills & Boon Reader Service, P.O. Box 236, Thornton Rd, Croydon, Surrey CR9 3RU, England. Readers in Southern Africa — write to: Independent Book Services Pty, Postbag X3010, Randburg, 2125, S. Africa.

Mills & Boon
the rose of romance

Mills & Boon

4 ROMANCES & 2 GIFTS - YOURS

ABSOLUTELY FREE!

An irresistible invitation from Mills & Boon! Please accept our offer of 4 free books, a pair of decorative glass oyster dishes and a special MYSTERY GIFT...Then, if you choose, go on to enjoy 6 more exciting Romances every month for just £1.35 each postage and packing free.

Send the coupon below at once to -
Reader Service, FREEPOST, P.O. Box 236, Croydon, Surrey CR9 9EL

✂ - - - - - - - - - - - - - - - *No stamp required* - - - - - - - - - - - - - -

YES! Please rush me my **4 Free Romances and 2 FREE Gifts !** Please also reserve me a Reader Service Subscription. so I can look forward to receiving 6 Brand New Romances each month, for just £8.10 total. Post and packing is **free**, and there's a free monthly Mills & Boon Newsletter. If I choose not to subscribe I shall write to you within 10 days - I understand I can keep the books and gifts whatever I decide. I can cancel or suspend my subscription at any time, I am over18.

EP60R

NAME _____

ADDRESS _____

_____

_____ *POSTCODE* _____

SIGNATURE _____

The right is reserved to refuse an application and change the terms of this offer. You may be mailed with other offers as a result of this application. Offer expires Dec 31st 1989 and is limited to one per household. offer applies in the UK and Eire only. Overseas send for details

mps MAILING PREFERENCE SERVICE